MOVIES, MAKEOVERS, AND BIG SURPRISES

best fr...

Stick Together. Friends' Forever!™

First published by Parragon in 2009

Parragon
Queen Street House
4 Queen Street
Bath BA1 1HE, UK

For other great BFC INK™ products check out our website at www.bfcink.com

© 2009 Parragon Books Ltd.
BFC INK.™ is a trademark of MGA in the U.S. and other countries.
All logos, names, characters, likenesses, images, slogans,
and packaging appearance are the property of MGA.
16300 Roscoe Blvd.
Van Nuys, CA 91406 U.S.A.
(800) 222-4685

All rights reserved. No part of this publication may be reproduced,
stored in a retrieval system, or transmitted, in any form or by any means,
electronic, mechanical, photocopying, recording, or otherwise,
without the prior permission of the copyright holder.

ISBN 978-1-4075-7860-6

Printed in U.S.A.

Please retain information for future reference.

Written by Becky Brookes, Rennie Brown, Sarah Delmege,
Kirsty Neale, and Caroline Plaisted

MOVIES, MAKEOVERS, AND BIG SURPRISES

PaRragon

Bath · New York · Singapore · Hong Kong · Cologne · Delhi · Melbourne

CONTENTS:

My Diary
by Aliesha

Saturday 3 pm

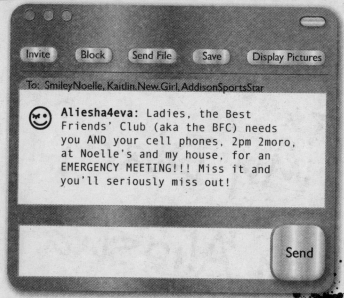

Invite | **Block** | **Send File** | **Save** | **Display Pictures**

To: SmileyNoelle, Kaitlin.New.Girl, AddisonSportsStar

😊 **Aliesha4eva:** Ladies, the Best Friends' Club (aka the BFC) needs you AND your cell phones, 2pm 2moro, at Noelle's and my house, for an EMERGENCY MEETING!!! Miss it and you'll seriously miss out!

Send

Sunday 5:35 pm

I've just had the worst BFC meeting EVER!

"Come in, come in!" I said earlier, opening the door and grabbing Addison's arm.

"What's the rush?" she grumbled.

"You'll see," I said. "Come on up!"

Noelle appeared at my shoulder. "Hey girls," she smiled.

6

Ever since me and my twin sis, Noelle, started the Best Friends' Club last summer with Calista and Addison, we've been holding regular meetings to discuss mega emergencies, such as how to raise cash to see The Beat Boyz in concert.

Kaitlin hasn't been in the club for very long. She joined the first week she arrived at our school, Green Meadow. But, in the short time she's been a member of the BFC, she's already changed the way our club looks. Check out Kaitlin's card designs below:

And of course Calista's moved to Canada, sob! But there's no reason why distance should separate BFs. OK, so it's sort of impossible for Calista to come to meetings. I just wish she didn't have to miss this one. It was really important...

Anyway, back to our club meeting.

"Right," I said. "This emergency meeting of the BFC is finally in session. Noelle, if you'd like to take notes."

My twin waved her notepad at me. "Yes, boss," she grinned.

"As you all know, Mickey Dean is starring in his first teen movie—'The New Boy.'"

"You might have mentioned it a few times," laughed Kaitlin.

"Well, Radio Rock is giving away five tickets to see the premiere next Friday," I continued. "They're holding a contest at 5:30 pm. All we have to do is answer a simple question to prove we're Mickey Dean's biggest fans!"

Addison and Kaitlin jumped up and ran toward me, screaming. Noelle shook her head.

8

"But there are going to be thousands of girls trying to win those tickets," she said. "There's no guarantee we'll even get through to the radio station in the first place."

"Ah," I said, "that will be where the cells come in. Each of us will call the contest line, and I'll call from both my cell AND the landline. One of us is bound to get through, eventually."

Addison looked at me. "Genius," she grinned.

So, at 5:29 pm, we huddled around the radio. Everyone had their cells ready, and I had my cell PLUS the landline phone, waiting to hit dial.

"And now. . .your chance to win five tickets to see the premiere of 'The New Boy.' Start dialing . . . NOW!" said the host.

We hit the dial keys.

"Busy signal," said Addison.

"Me, too," said Noelle, hitting redial. Kaitlin did the same. "I wish Calista was here to help!" I clutched both phones to my ear. Silence. And then. . .

"It's RINGING!" I held my breath as a computerized voice said, "You've reached the contest line. Please hold."

♡#'s

"We have five lucky girls on the line," said the host. "One of them will be the proud owner of five tickets to the premiere of Mickey Dean's first ever movie, 'The New Boy.'"

I closed my eyes. Please let it be me.

"Who will it be?" asked the host. "Let's find out. Computer, please pick one of the lines at random."

My fingers were crossed so tightly I could hardly hold my phone.

"Line 4," said the host, after a long pause. "Hello, who's that?"

"Hello!" I said eagerly, just as a familiar voice let out a squeal across the airwaves into the room.

I stared at the others in disbelief. No way. It couldn't be. Not. . .

"Hello, this is Dina!"

But it was. Dina Hart. Dina, along with her four sidekicks, Sophie, Gianna, Kelly, and Mel, were the BFC's archrivals.

We sat in silence as the host asked Dina which band Mickey Dean was the lead singer of. Even a complete no-hoper like Dina couldn't get that wrong. And she didn't. I put my cell down and switched off the radio. Dina and her cronies would be going to the premiere of "The New Boy" while we, the BFC, stayed home. Phooey!

Monday 5 pm

Obviously, Dina was the first person I bumped into this morning. She was standing with her pals outside the classroom, and as soon as they saw me they started discussing the premiere. Loudly. "I don't even like The Beat Boyz that much," Dina bragged. "I should sell the tickets on e-Bay."

Suddenly, Dina caught my eye and winked.

"Or maybe I should give them to a real Beat Boyz fan, like Aliesha here." She put her arm around my shoulder. "I bet you'd love to go, wouldn't you?"

"Of course," I said. "That would be amazing."

Wow, maybe I'd misjudged Dina, maybe she was a really nice girl, just waiting for the right opportunity to show it. . .

"Dream on," she burst out laughing, pushing me away. "Like that's ever going to happen."

11

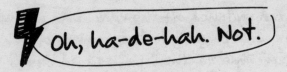

Oh, ha-de-hah. Not.

Wednesday 7:33 pm

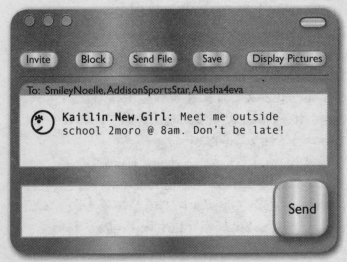

Invite | Block | Send File | Save | Display Pictures

To: SmileyNoelle, AddisonSportsStar, Aliesha4eva

Kaitlin.New.Girl: Meet me outside school 2moro @ 8am. Don't be late!

Send

Thursday 4:05 pm

This morning, before school, we met outside the school gates. Kaitlin was bouncing up and down with some exciting news.

12

Kaitlin grinned, reaching into her bag. "My older sister, Katie, is writing a review of 'The New Boy' for 'The Juice' magazine and she gave me these last night. Three tickets for the premiere!"

We all started jumping up and down, screaming.

"But wait a minute," I said. "There are only three tickets. And there are four of us."

"I know," said Kaitlin. "But that's all Katie could get. Aliesha, as Mickey's biggest fan, you should go. I think the rest of us need to draw straws. I brought some with me." She handed three straws of different lengths to me. "There's one short straw and two long. A long straw equals a ticket to the premiere."

"Sounds good," said Addison. Noelle nodded.

"Well, if you're sure," I said, holding the straws behind my back. I gave them a good shuffle, and held them out.

Addison went first. She pulled out a long straw and squealed with excitement.

Noelle went next and pulled out the short straw. "Oh, well," she smiled. If I'd drawn the short straw, I would have had a huge hissy fit. Whereas, my sister took the news with her usual good grace.

Kaitlin looked sheepish. "I guess I get the other long straw," she said, pulling it out. "Sorry, Noelle." "You won, fair and square," Noelle shrugged, smiling. "At least I got to choose, which is more than Calista did."

We all hugged, but it was hard to feel blissfully happy knowing two of the BFs wouldn't be coming to the premiere. Noelle looked sad enough and she's Noelle. . .How on earth will I tell Calista?

Wednesday 9 pm

So, I emailed Calista yesterday to tell her the good news. No reply. She must be really upset. . .

Thursday 5 pm

OK, you are not going to believe this!

Guess who turned up on our doorstep, with Addison and Kaitlin jumping up and down like idiots?

Calista!

Noelle came rushing downstairs as soon as she heard the screaming. "What are you doing here?" Trust Noelle to think of asking the sensible question.

Calista was grinning. "We've moved back! For good! Dad hated his job!"

We squealed so loudly Mom had to come and tell us to quiet down. It's so amazing!

And something more amazing. Addison gave Calista her Mickey Dean ticket. Just like that. No argument. All she said was, "It's your welcome home present." She was hugging Calista so hard, Calista could hardly say thank you.

Saturday 11 am

I am still in heaven! Calista's back from Canada and the premiere was AMAZING! A car picked us up from Katie's house, courtesy of "The Juice." After a mass group hugging session, Noelle and Addison waved us off at the front door, before Dad took them back to our house.

"I hope they'll be okay," I said, on the way to the premiere.

"Me too," Calista agreed, "it was so cool that Addison gave me her ticket. She is, like, THE best friend EVER!"

I had a plan. "I'm gonna take photos of everything so they don't miss anything."

Good thing I had a new memory card in my phone! Especially since the first people to see us climb out were Dina and co. Their faces made a great picture! Ha!

"What are you doing here?" Dina said in disbelief.

"We have press passes," I grinned. "You never know, we might get the scoop on Mickey Dean, too."

The movie was awesome. A girl can never have enough close-ups of Mickey! As soon as the movie was over, Katie grabbed Mickey for an interview. Then she asked him if he'd mind meeting some of his fans. When she called us over, I thought I'd burst with excitement.

"It's a pleasure to meet you," said Mickey, his brown eyes smiling right into mine.

I swallowed hard. "I think you're great!" I stuttered.

"Thanks," he grinned.

Luckily, Katie asked him if she could take a photo of him with me, Kaitlin, and Calista for "The Juice." I almost passed out when Mickey put his arm around me.

"Wait till the girls see this!" whispered Calista, as the flash went off.

Oh, no! Noelle and Addison! In the excitement, I had forgotten all about them. What kind of a BF was I?

"Are you okay?" asked Mickey.

"No," I said, blinking back tears. Forgetting he was a super-famous-rock-star-turned-actor, I told him all about the BFC and how we'd tried to win tickets to the competition, and that Katie had got us three press passes, while Noelle and Addison had to wait at home.

"That's terrible," said Mickey. "Hang on. Give your sister a call and tell her I want to speak to her."

Shakily, I hit Noelle's number. She answered right away.

So I said: →

> Uh, Noelle. Someone wants to speak to you.

Mickey winked at me as I passed him my cell.

> Hi, Noelle. This is Mickey Dean. No, really it is. I can prove it to you. Aliesha told me you and Addison couldn't come to the premiere, but I'd like you to come as my special guests to the after-show party, along with your friends. What's your address? Okay, a car will be at your house soon.

He hung up, passed me back the phone, and gave me the most gorgeous grin EVER!

"I don't know what to say," I said, gaping at him like a goldfish. Seriously, SO not attractive.

"Well, The Beat Boyz are like a BFC to me," Mickey smiled. "We've had to put our next album on hold because of this film, but they are a hundred percent supportive of me wanting to be an actor. I honestly don't know where I'd be without them. So I understand the importance of best friends. And I think Noelle and Addison are lucky to have you as theirs."

He bent down and kissed me on the cheek. "See you at the party!" he said and walked off.

I stared after him as he disappeared into the crowd. See? Even Mickey Dean is in his own BFC. Clubs rock!

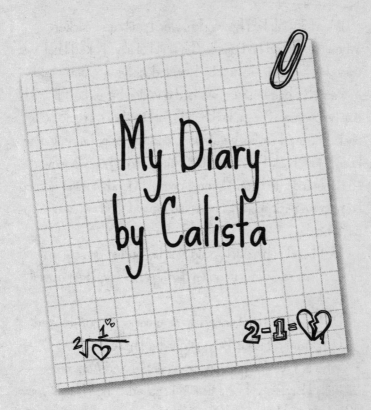

My Diary
by Calista

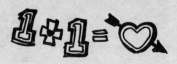

It's official. I'm the world's worst suitcase-packer. When we moved to Canada (I'm still totally stoked that we came back again—seriously, how indecisive are parents?), it wasn't so bad because we had a million boxes to fill with our belongings. But, now that I'm sitting here trying to pack for my family's week-long camping trip, I'm realizing I can't just pack EVERYTHING like I did when we moved to Canada. If it hadn't been for my friends coming around to help me pack, I probably would have filled my case with books.

"Definitely this skirt," said Kaitlin, pulling one out of my closet. "You can dress it down during the day, then glam it up at night."

"Do I need to be glammed up at a campground?" I asked.

"Duh," said Aliesha. "Boys might be there."

"Who is it you're going with again?" asked Addison.

"Sally Harris and her family," I replied. "She's Naomi's new best friend. Her mom suggested a camping trip to our mom, who thought it was a great idea. Next time Mom agrees to a camping trip, I'm taking you guys with me!"

"I'm totally NOT looking forward to this."

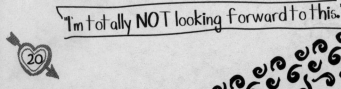

Saturday 5 pm

I'm SO going to miss my friends! We had such a cool time at Mickey Dean's movie premiere, it feels as if we're closer than ever. I promised to text them all the time and instant-message the minute I sniff out a computer on the campground. Addison thinks I'll love camping, but I'm not so sure. I have a funny feeling I'm in for a big surprise.

Sunday 7 pm

So, we're on vacation, the sun's shining, we're right next to the beach. What could go wrong?

EVERYTHING! We got here this afternoon, and the first thing I saw was a cool-looking coffee shop near the campground entrance with a sign in the window that said "Internet access." Yippee, I could IM my friends.

"It doesn't look as if the Harrises are here yet, Naomi," Mom said, pointing to the empty patch of grass next door to our camping spot. But just as we started to put up our tent, Sally and her family arrived. And THAT was when things started to go wrong. It turns out that little Sally's sister (like no one even told me she had one) is Gianna Harris.

See? I knew I was in for a big surprise. And not in a good way either.

Stuff to know about Gianna Harris

1. She goes to my school.
2. She's best friends with Dina.
3. She's originally from Ireland.
4. She moved in to our old house when we went to Canada.
5. She spread big fat lies at school about how bad the house smelled after we moved out.
6. She is the next-to-last person I would want to spend a camping trip with (the last one is Dina, obviously).

Monday 5 pm

This morning, Dad announced we were going to Branford Safari Park—all of us, including Gianna Harris. I actually really wanted to visit the park but no way was I up for going with Gianna.

22

"I'll stay here in the tent," I told Mom. "I've got some homework to do."

"Homework?" said Mom. "Not when we're on vacation."

So, I didn't have any choice except to go and spend the entire day making excuses to keep out of Gianna's way.

Calista Knight's tried and tested techniques for avoiding your enemy:

1. Hanging out in the gift shop.
2. Going to the bathroom.
3. Taking your little sister to the bathroom.
4. Taking your little sister's best friend to the bathroom.
5. Taking your little sister and her best friend to find the ice-cream truck.
6. Sitting in the car, reading your book.
7. Sitting in the bathroom, reading your book.

Tuesday 1 pm

I finally got the chance to sneak off to the campground coffee shop and use the Internet this morning. I was mega-desperate to let the others know what's been going on here.

23

Invite | Block | Send File | Save | Display Pictures

To: Aliesha4eva, SmileyNoelle, Kaitlin.New.Girl, AddisonSportsStar

Calista100: You will NOT believe who I'm on vacation with!

SmileyNoelle: Uh, your family.

Calista100: Besides them...

Aliesha4eva: Duh, Sally's family. Calista, if this is one of your made-up quizzes, it isn't a very good one.

Calista100: This is NO quiz, Aliesha. Guess who Sally's sister is??? Gianna HARRIS!

AddisonSportsStar: You're kidding?

Kaitlin.New.Girl: Oh, no! Poor you.

Calista100: Tell me about it. She keeps giving me these totally evil looks.

SmileyNoelle: We love you, even if Gianna Harris doesn't.

Kaitlin.New.Girl: And we really miss you.

Aliesha4eva: Sending you a big hug via cyberspace. IM us any time if you want 2 talk. x

Send

Wednesday 3 pm

Today has been the worst day **EVER**. It's karaoke night at the campground later and guess who has to go?! This is my worst nightmare. I might be a genius at math and science, but singing is **NOT** my bag. Luckily, Dad's the same.

"You and I are spectators only," he said, wrapping an arm around my shoulders. "Team Tone-Deaf," he explained to Mr. Harris. "Strictly no singing."

I vaguely heard Gianna snort with laughter, but I ignored her and grinned back at Dad.

Wednesday 8:30 pm �֎ ◇ ✖ ◇

Hello, good evening, and welcome to the most cringe-tastic moment of my entire life.

I knew something fishy was going on when Gianna kept smiling at me across the table, during karaoke.

When Gianna took her turn, singing The Beat Boyz hit, "Keep It Goin'," Mom leaned over and said to me, "She's really good, isn't she?" I made a face and tried to ignore Gianna's smug expression.

"Up next," announced the campground manager from the stage, "it's Calista Knight."

I froze, thinking I must have heard wrong.

"Calista Knight," called the manager. "That's you," hissed Naomi, nudging me in the ribs.

"Why's he saying my name?" I panicked, looking over at Dad.

And then I remembered. Gianna had overheard Dad tell Mr. Harris we were tone deaf. Gianna had put my name down to sing a karaoke song.

"Over here!" I heard her shout at the campground manager, and the next thing I knew, there was a dazzling bright spotlight shining in my face.

"No need to be shy," said the campground manager, who'd made his way over to our table.

"Ladies and gentlemen, Calista Knight," he announced, pushing me toward the microphone. The audience applauded, the music started, and I wondered if it was actually possible to die of embarrassment.

Gianna was sitting in the audience, smirking as I croaked my way through the song. It finally came to an end and there was a stunned kind of silence.

Then I heard a cheer, and someone clapping. It was Dad. Some people in the audience joined in too.

I ran across the room and headed toward our tent. I swear, if it's the last thing I do, I am going to get Gianna back for this.

Thursday 2 pm

Ha, I've got it! I've just been to the campground coffee shop again, and there was a poster on the door advertising a quiz later tonight. Gianna may have a good singing voice, but she's definitely not head of the class at school. And if she can put my name down for karaoke, I can enter her in the quiz. All I have to do now is convince Mom and Dad that we should all go. (Like they'll say no.)

Thursday 8:46 pm

I've just sent the BFC a text after a long IM-convo this morning about karaoke cringe.

So, obviously Mom and Dad agreed that the quiz night was a good idea.

■ **Message**

Mission revenge = Mission total success :-) C U soon!
C xxx

BACK   ☰   REPLY

"I'm so pleased you're finally getting into the spirit of things, Calista," Mom told me.

The campground manager was the quizmaster and he called each of the contestants up onto the stage to stand behind these little buzzer-stands. He looked a little alarmed when he saw me—I think he was worried I might sing again—but he wasn't half as shocked as Gianna when her name was called out. Seriously, you should have seen her face. She staggered up on stage, after being shoved forward by her parents (they obviously haven't noticed she's not the brightest).

The lights went down and we started answering the quiz questions. Or not, in Gianna's case. By the time the quiz was over, her score wasn't even in double figures. Me? I breezed it. Mom and Dad were so happy that I won. They've promised we can go to this huge fair in the next town tomorrow. Cool, but not quite as cool as seeing Gianna walk off stage wearing the prize for the loser of the competition—a T-shirt saying "Duh!" on the front.

Friday 10 am

Okay, so there have been some weird developments this morning.

I woke up really early and in a totally good mood. Mom, Dad, and Naomi were all still asleep, so I decided to go over to the campground coffee shop and instant-message Addison and co, to fill them in on last night's gossip.

Just as I sat down with my smoothie, a voice on the other side of the coffee shop made me jump.

"What are you doing here?" It was Gianna.

I shrugged. "E-mailing. Besides, I like it in here."

She snorted and took a slurp of her drink.

"I can't believe you entered me into that stupid quiz," snapped Gianna.

"Me?" I said. "What about you, putting my name down for karaoke? You know I can't sing."

"Yeah, well mine was more embarrassing," she said. "Sally's been saying 'Duh!' at every opportunity. It's driving me crazy."

"Naomi keeps singing in this really awful, croaky voice," I said, stirring my smoothie with a straw.

"Younger sisters are such a pain," said Gianna.

Gianna laughed, and before I knew it, we were chatting and giggling, trading little-sister stories.

"I'm sorry," she said, after a while. "About the karaoke."

"And I'm sorry about the quiz," I replied. "Truce?"

She nodded. "Truce."

We shook on it, kind of awkwardly, and then, still chatting, made our way back to the tents to hold my mom and dad to their promise about the fair. Which reminds me, I better go talk to them now...

Sunday 12 pm

The last few days have been seriously awesome. I can't believe I thought Gianna was horrible.

We had an amazing time at the fair on Friday, and spent all day yesterday on the beach, swapping MP3 players to listen to each other's fave songs.

She even asked me what it was like to meet Mickey Dean at his movie premiere (which was just the BEST, by the way).

When Aliesha first told Dina and her gang that we'd met Mickey, they all stormed off in a huff. But on vacation, without Dina by her side, Gianna wanted to hear all about it.

Then, last night, Mom and Dad took everyone out to a fancy restaurant. Me and Gianna had a total laugh picking our outfits and getting ready.

The only thing I feel a little bad about is the fact I really haven't done anything except hang out with Gianna since Friday. Not writing in my diary is one thing, but I haven't texted my BFC pals either.

To be honest, it's kind of difficult. Even though I know Gianna's cool, they don't. And she's still best friends with Dina. I'm not sure the others would understand our friendship.

It was so sad, packing our tent back into the car, then saying goodbye to Branford Bay and the Harrises.

Gianna gave me a huge hug, and said, "I'll text you," but neither of us mentioned school. I don't know what I'm going to tell the others when I see them later.

Sunday 8 pm

Being back with the BFC totally rocks!

We got together at Aliesha and Noelle's for a club meeting as soon I got back, and I gave them each the souvenirs I'd bought for them—a cute panda key ring from the safari park for Noelle, some funky shell beads for Kaitlin, a beach ball for Addison, and a glittery "superstar" pin for Aliesha.

They were dying to hear all about the quiz night. I felt totally bad after everything that's happened with Gianna, and I tried to tell the others that she's really okay.

"Anyone who hangs around with Dina is as bad as she is," Aliesha replied. "Just you wait, the minute we get back to school, Gianna will be back to her normal self."

Suddenly, I realized I wasn't going to risk ruining my old friendships for anything, not even for a cool new friend like Gianna. Maybe we can't be real friends at school, but at least we can stop being enemies. And then one day, who knows? There might be a way for all of us to get along.

MY DIARY BY ADDISON

FINALLY, Noelle and I saw Mickey Dean's movie, "The New Boy," at the cinema this afternoon. It seems like ages since the others watched it at the premiere.

Noelle and I have been putting our fingers in our ears and singing "la-la-la" to stop Aliesha, Kaitlin, and Calista from blabbing about the plot.

I still can't believe that Mickey sent a chauffeur to bring me and Noelle to the after-show party, though. It totally rocked. Although, not as much as meeting Mickey Dean himself. <u>SWOON!</u> I so get what Aliesha sees in him.

Mickey Dean's gorgeousness rating on screen = <u>a million out of ten.</u>

Boy I know closest to being as gorgeous as Mickey Dean = Ben Michelson.

Problem with Ben Michelson being so gorgeous = Noelle likes him, too.

SUNDAY 4·37 pm

UH-OH, CRISIS ALERT! I WAS AT THE SKATE PARK THIS MORNING WITH MY OLDER BROTHER, JAKE. WE MET BEN AND THEIR NEW FRIEND ELLIOT THERE. HE SEEMED PRETTY NICE, CUTE EVEN. BUT NOWHERE NEAR AS CUTE AS BEN.

I'D JUST BEEN SKATING AROUND, TRYING OUT A NEW TRICK I'D READ ABOUT IN "SKATE ON" MAGAZINE. ACTUALLY, I WAS QUITE PLEASED, COS I MANAGED NOT TO FALL DOWN, WHICH ALWAYS HAPPENS WHENEVER I TRY OUT A NEW STUNT.

ANYWAY, I WAS GETTING KIND OF TIRED, SO I SKATED OVER TO JOIN THE BOYS. THEY DIDN'T HEAR ME APPROACH AND WERE DEEP IN CONVERSATION. A CONVERSATION ABOUT GIRLS. A CONVERSATION THAT INCLUDED MOI!

A CONVERSATION IN WHICH BEN SAID (AND I QUOTE). . .

YOUR SISTER'S OKAY, JAKE, OKAY IN A HANGING-OUT FRIEND SORT OF WAY. BUT SHE'S NOT REALLY THE KIND OF GIRL THAT YOU'D ACTUALLY WANT TO GO OUT WITH ON A DATE, IS SHE? I MEAN, SHE'S NOT INTO GIRLY STUFF LIKE SOME OF HER FRIENDS.

OKAY, ADMITTEDLY, I DON'T REALLY DRESS UP MUCH OR WEAR LIP GLOSS, BUT THAT DOESN'T MEAN I CAN'T. I JUST CHOOSE NOT TO. BUT MAYBE I SHOULD TRY IT, JUST ONCE. JUST TO SEE IF I CAN BE GIRLY, TOO!

SUNDAY 7pm

To: Calista100, Aliesha4eva, SmileyNoelle, Kaitlin.New.Girl

AddisonSportsStar: Okay, don't laugh, but do you think you guys could give me a makeover?

Kaitlin.New.Girl: Yay! I thought you'd never ask.

Aliesha4eva: What took you so long?

SmileyNoelle: We're gonna make you look SO cute!

Calista100: Not that you don't now, of course. Seriously, you don't need to alter the way you look if you're happy with yourself.

AddisonSportsStar: I know, I just want a change.

Kaitlin.New.Girl: Come to my place after school 2moro for a BFC makeover.

Invite · Block · Send File · Save · Display Pictures

Send

Monday 8 pm

I had <u>NO</u> idea that skirts came in so many different shapes and sizes. Some were tiny mini-skirts (these belonged to Aliesha), some had sequins and designs (Kaitlin's, obviously), and others had frills (totally Noelle).

Not really my kind of thing, although I did sort of like one of Calista's denim skirts. It was mid-length with a sparkly sequined belt. Aliesha said it looked good when I tried it with one of Kaitlin's funky T-shirts.

Then Noelle got carried away and started plastering make-up on me. She dabbed some eye shadow on my lids and then glittery stuff around my cheeks. Plus some mascara and lip gloss. Noelle said I looked great but it was too much. I couldn't wait to get the stuff off. But I have to admit, the mascara did make my eyes look bigger. Aliesha said she thought I looked like a total babe. So did Kaitlin.

I'm just grateful that Calista was there! She said she thought it was a bit too much to wear all of the make-up at the same time and just lent me her mascara and a lip gloss. Phew!

Tuesday (after basketball practice)

I CAN'T BELIEVE WHAT HAS JUST HAPPENED. BASKETBALL WAS REALLY GOOD TONIGHT (I SCORED SIX POINTS) AND THE COACH SAID I MIGHT HAVE A PLACE IN THE TOURNAMENT LATER IN THE YEAR. BUT THAT'S NOT WHY I'M SO HAPPY.

IT ALL STARTED THIS MORNING WHEN MOM ASKED JAKE TO WALK ME HOME AFTER BASKETBALL. I KIND OF KNEW HE'D BE WITH BEN (SERIOUSLY, THOSE TWO DO EVERYTHING TOGETHER). SO I DECIDED TO TRY OUT MY BFC MAKEOVER AFTER PRACTICE. WHILE THEY WERE WAITING OUTSIDE THE LOCKER ROOMS FOR ME, I SLIPPED OUT OF MY GEAR AND INTO KAITLIN'S TOP, CALISTA'S DENIM SKIRT, AND ALIESHA'S GLITTERY PUMPS. THEN I PUT ON MY MASCARA AND LIP GLOSS, AND ADDED SUPER-CUTE FLOWERS IN MY HAIR.

"WHAT HAVE YOU BEEN DOING IN THERE?" JAKE ASKED ME WHEN I FINALLY APPEARED. "YOU TOOK AGES."

I CAN'T BELIEVE THAT JAKE MENTIONED NOTHING ABOUT MY NEW LOOK. NOTHING!!! LUCKILY, BEN DID.

"WOW, ADDISON! ARE YOU GOING TO A PARTY OR SOMETHING? YOU LOOK REALLY NICE," HE SAID.

"WHAT? THIS OLD THING?" I REPLIED, POINTING TO MY OUTFIT. "OH, NO! THIS IS JUST SOMETHING I'VE THROWN ON."

THROWN ON??? I CAN BE SUCH AN IDIOT SOMETIMES.
OBVIOUSLY, I HAVEN'T THROWN ANYTHING ON. BEN WILL SO
SEE THROUGH THAT.

"OH, QUIT IT—SHE JUST LOOKS LIKE SHE ALWAYS DOES,"
JAKE SNORTED, "A GEEK!"

FOR ONCE, I COULD HAVE HUGGED MY BROTHER. WE
INSULTED EACH OTHER MOST OF THE WAY HOME, WHICH
MEANT THAT I COULDN'T SAY ANY MORE EMBARRASSING
THINGS IN FRONT OF BEN. THANKFULLY!

WHEN WE GOT HOME, BEN LEFT ALMOST IMMEDIATELY.

"OH, WELL," I THOUGHT. "MAYBE MY MAKEOVER WASN'T
SO GOOD, AFTER ALL."

BUT THEN, I GOT THIS TEXT.

HAS BEN JUST ASKED
ME OUT ON A DATE?
HAS HE?
HAS HE???

Message

Do U want 2 go 4 swim on
Fri? 6pm? Ben

REPLY

Wednesday 4 pm

I'm dying to tell the others about Ben's text but how can I? I have to keep it a secret. Especially from Noelle. I didn't realize my makeover would actually get me a date with Ben. Really, I should just say "No!". I mean, I am breaking one of the BIGGEST rules of the Best Friends' Club, by keeping such a HUMONGOUS secret to myself. Not to mention the pact I made with Noelle about steering clear of Ben. But he's just so cute!!! Besides, no one will find out, right?

Thursday after school

Secrets are SO HARD TO KEEP! Every time I thought about Ben in school today, I couldn't help but smile. I didn't realize I was grinning like a lunatic, but Aliesha kept asking me what I was so pleased about.

Even Noelle almost guessed what was up.

"Hey, smiley," she said. "What's your secret?"

I told them I was just excited because I might be in a basketball tournament. I turned bright red. Telling fibs just doesn't feel right. But I can't tell them the truth. Not now, when I've kept it from them for TWO WHOLE DAYS! Plus, I'm seeing Ben tomorrow night...

Friday 8 pm

TOTAL DISASTER! EVERYTHING (AND I MEAN EVERYTHING) WENT WRONG. WHERE DO I START? OKAY...

1. I GOT DRESSED UP, MAKE-UP AND EVERYTHING, AND SHOWED UP AT THE POOL AFTER TELLING MOM THAT I WAS GOING SWIMMING WITH THE BFC. EEK! ANOTHER LIE.

2. I MET BEN, ONLY TO DISCOVER THAT HE WAS THERE WITH JAKE AND ELLIOT. DID BEN TELL ME THERE WERE GOING TO BE FOUR OF US? NO, HE DID NOT.

3. I DID MY LONGEST EVER UNDERWATER SWIM AND THOUGHT IT WAS QUITE IMPRESSIVE. THEN JAKE AND BEN BURST OUT LAUGHING WHEN I CAME UP FOR AIR. FINALLY, JAKE TOLD ME WHAT WAS SO FUNNY. I HAD BLACK EYES WHERE MY MAKE-UP HAD RUN. NO ONE TOLD ME YOU COULDN'T WEAR MAKE-UP IN SWIMMING POOLS, UNLESS IT WAS WATERPROOF. HOW WAS I SUPPOSED TO KNOW? SO I LOOKED LIKE A PANDA— ONLY NOT, ACCORDING TO JAKE, A CUTE ONE.

AND THEN IT GOT WORSE. AFTERWARDS, UPSTAIRS IN THE SNACK BAR, ELLIOT WAS IN THE MIDDLE OF TALKING TO ME ABOUT A NEW SKATEBOARDING STUNT HE'D BEEN TRYING TO DO, WHEN BEN INTERRUPTED US AND ASKED IF HE COULD TALK TO ME IN PRIVATE.

HE TOOK ME TO A CORNER, LEANED IN TOWARD ME (I SWEAR, I NEARLY FAINTED), AND WHISPERED, "UM, LISTEN ADDISON, THERE'S SOMETHING I'VE BEEN MEANING TO ASK YOU FOR A WHILE." HE SOUNDED NERVOUS. THIS WAS IT! BEN WAS FINALLY GOING TO ASK ME OUT. WHO KNEW A SIMPLE MAKEOVER WOULD TRANSFORM MY LIFE FOREVER?

"THIS IS A LITTLE EMBARRASSING," HE CONTINUED, "BUT I WONDERED IF YOU KNEW IF NOELLE LIKED ANYONE AT THE MOMENT."

HUH? NOELLE? WHY WOULD HE ASK ME THAT, UNLESS. . .

"ADDISON, IS THAT YOU?" IT WAS KAITLIN. SHE WAS THERE WITH HER DAD'S GIRLFRIEND, JEN, AND HER BABY BROTHER, BILLY. SHE LOOKED TOTALLY SHOCKED TO SEE ME. I MUST HAVE HAD A TOTALLY GUILTY LOOK ON MY FACE, BECAUSE SHE PULLED ME TO ONE SIDE AND ASKED, "IS SOMETHING GOING ON BETWEEN YOU AND BEN?"

I LOOKED DOWN AT MY SPARKLY PUMPS, FEELING ASHAMED. "IT'S NOT WHAT YOU THINK, KAITLIN. . ." I BEGAN, QUIETLY.

SUDDENLY KAITLIN GASPED. "IS THAT WHY YOU WANTED A MAKEOVER? IT IS, ISN'T IT? OH, ADDY, WHAT ABOUT NOELLE? YOU MADE A PACT."

I FEEL TERRIBLE. HOW COULD I HAVE BEEN SO STUPID? I'D PUT A BOY BEFORE ONE OF MY BEST FRIENDS.

A BOY WHO DOESN'T EVEN LIKE ME!!! WELL, NOT LIKE-ME LIKE-ME, ANYWAY. BEFORE I COULD TRY AND EXPLAIN THINGS TO KAITLIN, SHE'D RUSHED DOWN THE STEPS TO THE POOL'S LOCKER ROOMS.

Saturday morning

THIS IS OFFICIALLY THE WORST DAY EVER! I WENT OVER TO KAITLIN'S THIS MORNING. I WANTED TO EXPLAIN. TOO LATE! NOELLE WAS THERE ALREADY. THEY STARED AT ME LIKE I WAS ONE OF DINA'S PALS. I TRIED TO APOLOGIZE BUT NOELLE JUST SNAPPED, "SO YOU ASKED ME TO HELP MAKE YOU OVER SO YOU COULD GET BEN'S ATTENTION?" I'VE NEVER HEARD HER SOUND SO MAD.

THEN KAITLIN JOINED IN. "YOU'RE A SNEAK, ADDISON!"

I WAS TOO UPSET TO EXPLAIN ANY MORE. I RAN ALL THE WAY HOME. JAKE WANTED TO KNOW WHY I WAS CRYING, BUT I JUST PUSHED PAST HIM AND HAVE BEEN HIDING IN MY ROOM EVER SINCE. THEY'RE RIGHT. I AM A SNEAK. I SHOULD HAVE BEEN HONEST INSTEAD OF GOING BEHIND NOELLE'S BACK!

Sunday evening

I TOLD CALISTA WHAT HAPPENED AND SHE WAS LIKE TOTALLY "UH-OH!" SHE DIDN'T TAKE SIDES OR ANYTHING BUT I COULD TELL THAT SHE COMPLETELY UNDERSTOOD WHY THEY WERE SO UPSET. I GAVE HER BACK HER MASCARA AND LIP GLOSS. I AM NEVER GOING TO BE GIRLY AGAIN.

Monday evening

SCHOOL WAS TRICKY. NOELLE AND KAITLIN WEREN'T MEAN OR ANYTHING, BUT THEY WERE ACTING LIKE I WAS HARDLY THERE. I COULD TELL CALISTA AND ALIESHA WEREN'T SURE WHAT TO DO.

Invite   Block   Send File   Save   Display Pictures

To: SmileyNoelle, Kaitlin.New.Girl, AddisonSportsStar

Aliesha4eva: Emergency BFC Meeting. At my house. After school. All members must attend unless they are completely and utterly dead.

Send

Tuesday 5 pm

OK, SO I DIDN'T WANT TO GO TO THE MEETING. I KNEW NOELLE AND KAITLIN WOULD BE SITTING THERE, STARING AT ME. AND THEY WERE.

OF COURSE, ALIESHA GOT STRAIGHT TO THE POINT. "THREE OF OUR BFs ARE ON THE OUTS WITH EACH OTHER AND THAT'S AGAINST THE RULES. WE HAVE TO FIX IT. NOW!"

I DECIDED IT WAS BEST TO APOLOGIZE RIGHT AWAY. "I'M SORRY. I JUST WANTED BEN TO LIKE ME. AND IT WAS SNEAKY OF ME, NOT TELLING YOU BECAUSE I KNOW YOU LIKE HIM TOO." I LOOKED AT NOELLE AND I COULD SEE SHE WAS LISTENING. "THE TRUTH IS HE ONLY ASKED ME OUT TO FIND OUT IF YOU LIKED HIM."

NOELLE TURNED RED AS A BEET WHEN I SAID THAT.

"I'VE BEEN SUCH AN IDIOT," I SAID. "THERE'S NO WAY I WOULD LET A BOY COME BETWEEN US EVER AGAIN."

"OH, ADDY," NOELLE BEAMED, HUGGING ME. "I'VE MISSED YOU. BESIDES, I CAN'T STAY MAD AT YOU FOR LONG."

ALIESHA SUGGESTED THAT I READ THE BFC PLEDGE OUT LOUD, JUST SO WE COULD ALL HEAR THE PROMISES AGAIN. I MEAN, IT'S BEEN A WHILE SINCE KAITLIN READ THEM FOR HER TRUE AND TOTAL FRIENDSHIP TEST WHEN SHE

FIRST JOINED THE CLUB. SO I DID—TO PROVE HOW
MUCH MY BFs MEAN TO ME.

"THE BEST FRIENDS' CLUB PLEDGE," I BEGAN. "AS
MEMBERS OF THE BEST FRIENDS' CLUB WE SOLEMNLY SWEAR
TO ABIDE BY THE FOLLOWING SET OF RULES. WE PROMISE TO...

1. ALWAYS BE LOYAL TO THE CLUB.
2. NEVER SPILL ANY SECRETS (WELL, NOT
   ON PURPOSE ANYWAY).
3. SETTLE ANY ARGUMENTS SENSIBLY AND CALMLY.
4. MAKE LIFE IN OUR CLUB FUN, FUN, FUN!
5. NEVER LEAVE ANY CLUB MEMBERS OUT.
6. ALWAYS TELL THE TRUTH, THE WHOLE TRUTH,
   AND NOTHING BUT THE TRUTH.
7. TREAT EACH OTHER WITH RESPECT.
8. NEVER LET A BOY GET IN THE WAY OF
   FRIENDSHIP.
9. ALWAYS BE THERE FOR EACH OTHER.
10. REMEMBER BFF (BEST FRIENDS FOREVER).

WE ENDED UP HAVING A MASS GROUP HUG WHEN I FINISHED.

 THE BFC IS SO FOREVER!

My diary
by Noelle

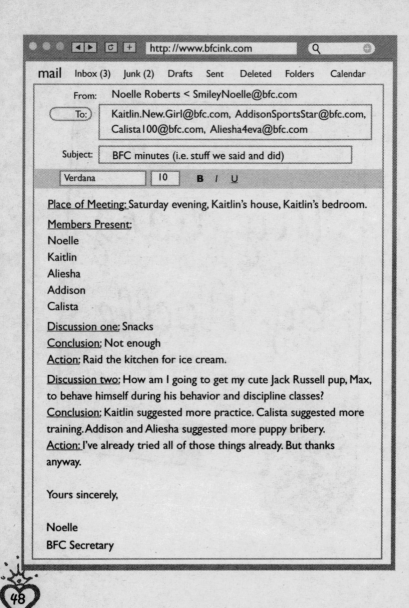

http://www.bfcink.com

From: Noelle Roberts < SmileyNoelle@bfc.com

To: Kaitlin.New.Girl@bfc.com, AddisonSportsStar@bfc.com, Calista100@bfc.com, Aliesha4eva@bfc.com

Subject: BFC minutes (i.e. stuff we said and did)

Verdana   10   **B** *I* <u>U</u>

<u>Place of Meeting:</u> Saturday evening, Kaitlin's house, Kaitlin's bedroom.

<u>Members Present:</u>

Noelle

Kaitlin

Aliesha

Addison

Calista

<u>Discussion one:</u> Snacks

<u>Conclusion:</u> Not enough

<u>Action:</u> Raid the kitchen for ice cream.

<u>Discussion two:</u> How am I going to get my cute Jack Russell pup, Max, to behave himself during his behavior and discipline classes?

<u>Conclusion:</u> Kaitlin suggested more practice. Calista suggested more training. Addison and Aliesha suggested more puppy bribery.

<u>Action:</u> I've already tried all of those things already. But thanks anyway.

Yours sincerely,

Noelle

BFC Secretary

Sunday 6.50 pm ♡

I wish everyone at Max's behavior and discipline class could see him now. He looks so sweet when he's asleep at the foot of my bed. He hardly looks like the kind of puppy who would chew holes in somebody's pants.

It really is a shame that the strictest dog trainer in the world is such a dedicated fan of flared pants. I mean, the sight of Ms. Loop's billowy pants swaying in the breeze would catch the eye of any puppy. You can't exactly blame Max for wanting a closer look. He was just doing some doggy detective work. I just wish he hadn't detected quite so much with his teeth, if you know what I mean!

When you think about it, it doesn't say much for Ms. Loop's behavior and discipline classes, if she can't keep the puppies from eating her clothes. I just don't know what's gotten into Max recently. He was doing so well, but a few weeks ago he went into nibble mode.

The thing is, the Brookbanks Dog Rescue Center, the animal shelter where I volunteer on weekends (and first fell in love with Max) is putting on a show in a week and I've already entered Max into loads of competitions. But after today's chew-a-thon, Ms. Loop (a judge at the show) told me that she didn't think Max would be good enough for any of the competitions.

Monday 5:45 pm

I told Addison about the pants episode today and she almost choked on her sports drink.

"Maybe he'll grow up to be a fashion police dog," she spluttered, laughing. "Those flared pants sound pretty hideous."

"He roams the streets, day and night," I said dramatically, "searching out bad fashion wherever he goes."

"When he finds it, he shows no mercy," Addison continued in a deep voice. "For he is a fashion police dog and he is trained to do a job."

HA! HA! HA! Aaaww! You've got to love Addison! I'm so glad everything is cool again between us.

At first, I was upset about her "date" with Ben, but best friends forgive each other. I mean, if friends don't forgive each other then nobody would stay friends for long, would they?

Anyway, in spite of what Addison says, I don't think Ben REALLY likes me. I think he was just trying to find out if I wanted to be his friend. How can Ben, a totally hot guy, have a crush on someone like me? Uh-uh! No way.

Tuesday 7:56 pm

NO WAY! NO WAY! NO WAY!

Development Number One:
I found a note in class today.
Guess what it said! ➡

> Ben Michelson likes Noelle.

Can you believe it?
I have several questions:
A) Who wrote it?
B) Is it true?
C) IS IT TRUE?????????????????

Okay. The likely answer is "No." I found the note on the floor by Dina's desk and since she knows I like Ben, it's got to be a trick, hasn't it? Aargh! The whole boy thing is sooo complicated! It's GOT to be one of Dina's sick jokes.

Development Number Two:

I ACTUALLY MANAGED TO TEACH Max TO SIT AND STAY TODAY!!! He was so good! He waited until I called him and everything. I'm so excited!

Maybe this means that he'll behave himself at the show after all. It's not that I want to win any prizes or anything (although that would be SO cool). I just want everybody to see how gorgeous and amazing Max is, that's all.

Wednesday 7:30 pm

Number of days to the Brookbanks Dog Show: Three.
                              So exciting!

Number of rumors about Ben liking me: None.

(See! I knew it couldn't be true.)

Number of things that Max has chewed: None.

Yay!

Ms. Loop ran a midweek behavior and discipline class tonight because so many of her "special pupils" (her words, not mine) are competing in the Brookbanks show. After Max's behavior on Sunday, I thought she might not let us train again, but it was almost as if she'd forgotten the whole incident. She stood at the door of the community center, beaming in a blindingly bright pink and orange suit. Some of the younger puppies were actually too frightened to go in.

Inside, Ms. Loop snapped into action. "Alright-y! Let's see which of my special puppies has learned to sit and stay," she boomed.

I nervously raised my hand.

"Max can," I squeaked. Ms. Loop practically fainted in surprise when Max did it at my command.

"What an improvement!" she yelled at the top of her voice. "Good job, Max. I hope this is the kind of behavior we can expect at the show."

So do I, Ms. Loop. Believe me, so do I.

Thursday 6 pm

Number of days to the Dog Show: Two.

Number of rumors about Ben liking me: None. Dina is mean.

Number of things that Max has chewed: None. La, la, la, Max rules!

Friday 8:15 pm

Aargh, it's showtime tomorrow. I keep looking at Max to see if he seems any naughtier than normal, but it's just so hard to tell. I think he looks cute all the time, even when he's chewing up my favorite T-shirt.

Saturday 9 am

Look what Leanne sent me in the mail. She's SO sweet! Leanne works at Brookbanks as a dog handler. When I first started volunteering at the rescue center, she gave me loads of great tips.

Dear Noelle and Max,
You'll always be Brookbanks champs no matter what! Look for me at the show.
Love, Leanne x
P.S. I'm one of the judges!

54

She was really supportive when I adopted Max and she helped Ben adopt his rescue dog, Sam, too.

⭐ Saturday 6:20 pm ⭐

Okay, so we got to Brookbanks and made our way to the practice area before the competitions began. I was just putting Max through his obedience routine when a miniature mass of hair and teeth zoomed into the enclosure and tried to nip Max on the tail.

"Oh, so sorry," drawled a familiar voice.

I turned around to see Dina and her crew, cackling by the gate. I scooped up Max and turned my back on them. I wasn't going to let Dina and her yappy little terrier ruin my day. I marched off angrily in the direction of the show ring and bumped slap-bang into a boy-shaped object.

"What's up, Noelle?" asked Ben, gorgeously.

So yes, there was Ben. Ben and Sam. At the show. The funny thing was, I didn't get a chance to be shy. I was too fired up about Dina and her bully of a terrier. I started telling Ben all about it. He is a totally good listener, by the way.

Then suddenly we heard an announcement over the loudspeakers.

"Hey, it's the obedience trials," said Ben. "Come on."

I followed Ben and Sam through the crowds. When we reached the show ring, we spotted Leanne on the judges' stage.

"Go get 'em, Max! You can do it, Sam!" she cheered as we went past.

Things started off really well. When Max sat on my command, Kaitlin and Addison cheered like crazy and Calista and Aliesha waved their hot dogs in encouragement.

And that's when it all went wrong. Max shot across the ring and disappeared into the crowd to see the BFC girls. Two seconds later, he appeared with Aliesha's hot dog in his mouth. The other dogs and puppies in the ring went INSANE! They all raced after Max and the hot dog in a blur of tails and tongues.

Sam was the only dog who stayed still.

Ben must be like a dog whisperer or something.

Suddenly Max jumped up on the judges' stage and dropped the hot dog at Ms. Loop's feet.

"No way! I think Max's trying to give it to her as a present," chuckled Ben. Eek, so embarrassing!

Ms. Loop took out a handkerchief and picked up the hot dog with a look of distaste. Max then bounded over to Leanne, who patted him on the head.

"Don't worry about old Loopy," whispered Leanne, when I went over to get Max. "Her sense of humor is nonexistent. Don't take it personally. Now try and calm Max down a little, okay?"

I nodded gratefully and took Max to a quiet corner until the next competition.

I won't go into details, but let's just say that the next few competitions didn't go as planned. When the time came to award the prizes, I felt totally depressed.

"As if Max will actually win anything," Dina said, as we all lined up. "Hope you liked your little luhhwe note about Ben, by the way." She flounced off, her terrier yapping at her side.

As the prizes were handed out, I began to drift into a daydream, thinking that maybe one day Max would win a prize. Suddenly, I looked up at the judges and spotted Leanne grinning like crazy.

"I repeat, the prize for the waggiest tail goes to Max," boomed Ms. Loop, a little reluctantly.

I climbed up on stage with Max, and Leanne attached a big ribbon to his collar. Everyone in the crowd was cheering and clapping.

"They loved the thing with the hot dog. Best part of the show, if you ask me," whispered Leanne.

Saturday 6:30 pm

Guess who just called me! Guess! Guess! **Ben Michelson!!!** Guess what he said! Guess! Guess!

Okay, I know it's not because he likes me or anything, but he's offered to help me train Max!!! He figures that Sam might have a calming influence!!! We're getting together tomorrow morning!!!!!!!!!!!!!!!!!!

 Hmm. I wonder what I should wear!

58

My Diary

by Kaitlin

Aw! Noelle just told me the news about Ben.
He hasn't actually asked her out on a real date or
anything. But the fact that he wants to help her train
little Max for future puppy competitions is a <u>MAJOR</u>
hint that he likes her, right?

How exciting!!! Our very own BFC romance. Maybe
they'll get married. Gasp, maybe I'll finally be a
bridesmaid!!! Well, okay so Noelle and Ben aren't
actually together-together yet. Especially since Noelle
refuses to even acknowledge that Ben has a crush on
her. But still, there's a bigger chance of those two
getting together than my glam, older sister, Katie. I've
been waiting for her to get hitched to a hottie for ages.
Not that a potential future husband is on the horizon...

"Not this again," Katie groaned, when I last
mentioned the "b" word to her ("b" for bridesmaid,
that is). "If I ever get married, and that's a big IF,
I'm not sure I'll even have bridesmaids. Seriously,
Kaitlin, do you want to walk down the aisle in a hideous,

puffball dress? I don't, that's for sure." Hmm, she has a point...

Wait, gotta go... Dad's calling me.

Uh-oh! He's asked Katie to come over for dinner. Apparently, he has some big news!!!

The only times Dad has ever called for a family meeting were to:

a) introduce us to Jen when they first started dating and **b)** announce they were having a baby, two years later. Which was cool. Our little step-bro, Billy, is so cute. But what if it's bad news this time? What if they're planning on moving away, like Calista and her family did? Okay, so they came BACK, but I don't want to move. I'm happy here.

Things I love about my life:
* Being in the Best Friends' Club
* Being the official Club Designer in the BFC
* Going to my school, Green Meadow (except for Dina the Diva and co. being there too, obviously)
* Having a crush on Addison's hot older brother, Jake

sunday 7 pm ❀ ❀ ❀ ❀ ❀ ❀

Invite   Block   Send File   Save   Display Pictures

To: Calista100, Aliesha4eva, SmileyNoelle, AddisonSportsStar

Kaitlin.New.Girl: Dad's just dropped the biggest bombshell EVER!!!

SmileyNoelle: What? WHAT? Spill.

Kaitlin.New.Girl: Dad and Jen are engaged!

Calista100: That's great news. Congratulations! Aren't you happy?

Kaitlin.New.Girl: I guess I should be. He and Jen have asked me and Katie to be bridesmaids.

Aliesha4eva: Wait, that's great, isn't it? Haven't you been dying to be a bridesmaid since, like, ever?

Kaitlin.New.Girl: Yeah, but at Katie's wedding not Dad's! Dad said that the date's set for a week from Saturday. I'm not sure I'm ready 4 a stepmom that soon!

Send

62

"Wow! That's less than two weeks away," Katie calculated, after Dad and Jen broke the news to us. "What's the big rush?"

"Well," Dad began, "Jen and I are happy together and we don't see the point of waiting any longer."

"I suppose," Katie shrugged. "But I hope you realize that doesn't give me long to plan my outfit."

"Actually," Jen added nervously, turning to me, "we wondered if you and Katie would be our bridesmaids. Billy will be the ring bearer, of course."

Bridesmaid? "If you want." I guess I didn't sound very excited. Of course there was no way I wanted to hurt Jen's feelings but it was all feeling kind of rushed.

I think Katie must have been feeling the same way because she said, "Um, you really think we'll find bridesmaid dresses in just 13 days?"

"There's a lovely bridal shop in town," Jen continued, after seeing the panic-stricken look on Katie's face. "We'll just pick the best dresses they have in stock."

monday 7 pm

Okay, so it's not just Katie who's worried about what we're going to be wearing. And it's not just the dresses. I like Jen. But things will change once she's my stepmom. I know they will. And Jen is so different from me. Which she totally proved this afternoon...

After school, I met Jen and Katie at Bride2Be, the bridal shop in town. Total disaster!

For starters, "blush" is Jen's color theme. So we tried on a LOT of pink dresses. We were just being zipped up into the only pink numbers left in the shop—a pair of matching puff-tastic outfits (flowery sleeves and flared skirt)—when Jen clapped her hands together and shouted, "Perfect, I love them."

I looked at Katie in horror. We looked hideous.

"Are we looking at the same dress here?" I asked Jen sarcastically. "We can't wear these!"

"Come on, Kaitlin," Katie whispered. "It's Dad and Jen's special day. We only have to wear the dresses once."

But I wasn't convinced. "I'm sorry, Jen," I said. "I just don't think being a bridesmaid is really...me."

tuesday 5:45 pm

Dad isn't too pleased. I mean, he's trying to be nice and everything, but he's just spent an HOUR trying to persuade me to go along with the whole bridesmaid thing. He thinks it's just the dress and of course I didn't want to upset him more by telling him it was the WHOLE wedding and stepmom thing.

wednesday 8 pm

I've just been downstairs to get a drink, and I overheard Dad and Jen talking about the wedding.

"I was really looking forward to seeing my three favorite girls walking down the aisle toward me," I heard Dad tell Jen. "You, Katie, and Kaitlin."

"It doesn't matter," Jen replied, putting an arm around Dad. "Kaitlin will be there supporting you, whether she's a bridesmaid or not."

"I know," Dad sighed. "It's just not how I imagined our wedding day to be..."

Duh! Did he really think we were going to be the Perfect Family just like that? He could have given us a bit more warning.

(friday 7 pm)

I hardly spoke at the BFC meeting today.

"Okay," Aliesha said at last. (I'd been sitting on her bed staring out the window while the BFC was trying to compose a fan letter to Mickey Dean.) "What's up, Kait?"

Everyone was staring at me, looking worried. Noelle came and sat next to me and put her arm around me. "You're not exactly the noisiest member of the BFC, but you're not usually THIS quiet." She gave me a sympathetic squeeze. "What's wrong?"

That's when it all came out. About how I was worried about having Jen as an actual, real-life stepmom.

"But you liked her when she was just your Dad's girlfriend," Calista pointed out.

"She hasn't changed, has she?" Addison sounded worried.

I shrugged. "I guess not. But how many other people make their bridesmaids dress up as puffballs?"

"Loads!" Aliesha grinned. "Why else do you think the bridal shop sells such gross outfits?"

Okay, she had a point. But I still wasn't convinced. "I don't want Jen to be my stepmom, so why should I be a bridesmaid at their stupid wedding?"

Noelle, Addison, Calista, and Aliesha just looked at each other.

"All right," Addison said at last. "The BFC needs to come up with a plan."

sunday 8 pm

Some plan! Going to Dad and telling him how I feel about the wedding! With friends like that, who needs enemies? It was Aliesha's idea. Of course. She and Noelle went to talk to Dad while Addison and Calista took me to the skate park.

They didn't warn me what they were planning. Not till it was too late.

"Aliesha's doing what?" I screamed at Addison when she confessed why they'd lured me away from the house.

"We thought it would help," Calista shrugged. But I hardly heard her. I was racing for home, praying I was in time to stop the BFC from ruining my life.

Too late!

Dad looked like someone had dropped a hundred-ton weight on his head, and Jen's eyes were red as if she'd been crying. Aliesha and Noelle were just standing there looking dumb. Some BFs they are!

Then of course Katie phoned as soon as she heard to have HER say. "Why couldn't you and your friends keep quiet? Now everyone's upset. I can't believe you're trying to spoil Dad's wedding!"

Could I feel any worse?

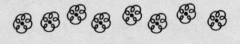

monday 8 am

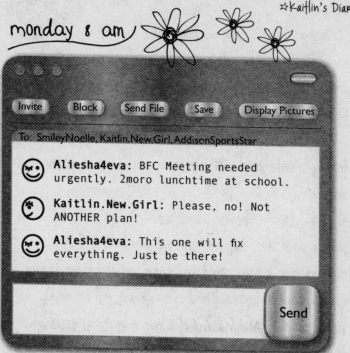

To: SmileyNoelle, Kaitlin.New.Girl, AddisonSportsStar

Aliesha4eva: BFC Meeting needed urgently. 2moro lunchtime at school.

Kaitlin.New.Girl: Please, no! Not ANOTHER plan!

Aliesha4eva: This one will fix everything. Just be there!

Send

tuesday 8 pm

Okay, so it wasn't THE worst idea. Aliesha felt so bad about her last plan backfiring, she persuaded the BFC to organize the best engagement party ever for Dad and Jen. After school, they decorated our living room with balloons and streamers and brought cake and sandwiches and soda and put a huge banner saying

"Congratulations" across the door.

"I know you're not happy," Aliesha told me before Dad and Jen got home from work. "But making everyone else unhappy isn't going to help."

I raised my eyebrows and gave her a look, as if to say "And exactly WHO was it who'd made them unhappy?"

"OK, OK," Aliesha admitted. "My last idea wasn't such a good one. But this one will work. We'll get everyone in a good mood and then you just have to say you'll be a bridesmaid and everything will be okay."

What else could I do? Katie was right. It wasn't fair to spoil Dad's big day.

So, while Dad was busy stuffing his face with cake, I told Jen to get the dresses for me and Katie. She was so happy it was almost worth it. She asked me to keep it as a surprise for Dad. So I only told Katie and she totally forgave me.

Of course, I'm glad everyone's happy, but it doesn't change how I feel. I guess I'll just have to get used to it...

wednesday 5 pm

Well, maybe I've been wrong about Jen.

She knocked on my bedroom door after school and asked to talk. I knew it was serious because she was carrying the bridesmaid dresses.

"Look," she began. "I know it's scary. Having someone new in your family. Permanently." Well at least she understood that much. "But you got used to Billy, didn't you?" she reminded me.

Actually, I like Billy a lot. I couldn't imagine NOT having him in our family.

"You're good at sewing," she went on. "Why don't you help me alter these dresses the way YOU'd like them."

I looked at the pile of pink frills and puffs. "That's going to be a LOT of work," I said. "And the wedding's on Saturday."

"Can't we get your friends to help us?" Jen suggested.

Of course! What a great idea! Maybe Jen isn't a total alien after all.

The past couple of days have been so manic...

Jen and the BFC spent HOURS customizing the outfits, based on my design. The puffy sleeves went and we turned the dresses into Grecian-style gowns. I totally loved them!!!

Jen loved them too. She invited my BFC pals to the reception. And we managed to keep everything a secret from Dad, right up until the point when Katie and I walked down the aisle, as Jen's bridesmaids. He was SO choked up, and even got a little misty-eyed. Awwww.

Later, at the party, Jake and Ben turned up. Ben dragged Noelle onto the dance floor for a slow dance. Then Jake asked me (yes, ME) if I wanted to dance too!!! I have to say though, it is totally embarrassing to dance with a BOY in front of your dad and your big sister. Cringe-orama. I caught Addison making kissy faces at me behind Jake's back. Which kind of ruined the moment a little. Still, the dance was SO worth it. Swoon! I LOVE being a bridesmaid.

My Diary

by Aliesha

I knew today was going to be a good day. Not only did the latest issue of "The Juice" (aka the best magazine in the history of the world) come out, but it had a pull-out, full-size poster of Mickey Dean. I mean, totally gorgeous or what?

I couldn't wait to show the girls. We've become even bigger fans of The Beat Boyz since we met Mickey at the premiere of his film, "The New Boy." And let me just say, those legendary chocolate-brown eyes are even more yummy in real life. Swoon!

Anyway, I hurried into our classroom and grinned at Noelle, who was already sitting at her desk, checking her math homework. Except, she wasn't really. She had this dreamy expression on her face.

"I just can't seem to concentrate on these equations," she sighed.

I rolled my eyes at her. "You're not still thinking about your little dance with Ben at Kaitlin's dad's wedding, are you?"

Noelle nodded her head.

"Well, this will take your mind off it," I added, waving my magazine in front of her. "The latest copy of 'The Juice.'"

Noelle made a face. "Aliesha, there's more to life than just pop groups and makeovers."

"Obviously," I grinned. "There's hanging out with the BFC, having manicures, going to concerts, shopping at the mall. . .I could go on!"

"Sometimes I wonder how we're related," Noelle muttered, turning to her math homework again.

"So, you don't want to check out the latest gossip on The Beat Boyz?" I grinned, pointing to their article in "The Juice."

"Oh, all right," Noelle laughed, reaching for it.

The day got even better. After attendance, we trooped into assembly.

"Good morning, everyone," said Mr. Chester, the principal. "I've got some exciting news for you. This Friday, after school, we will be putting on our very own Green Meadow Talent Contest. Not only that, but Chris Adams will make a special guest appearance as one of the judges."

My mouth gaped open in disbelief. Chris Adams was huge! He'd discovered loads of really cool bands, including The Beat Boyz. And now he was coming to Green Meadow School!!!

Mr. Chester continued. "I am putting a sign-up sheet on the school bulletin board tomorrow, so make sure you put your name down if you want to enter. Oh, and before I forget, the winner will get to record a song in a real recording studio and win one hundred dollars."

I have to win that prize! Not just for the money—although that would be amazing—but to record a song!!! I can see my name in lights:

Teen sensation!

Superstar in the making!

Aliesha ROBERTS

Discovered in school talent contest!

Monday 6 pm

(Invite) (Block) (Send File) (Save) (Display Pictures)

To: SmileyNoelle, Calista100, Kaitlin.New.Girl, AddisonSportsStar

Aliesha4eva: Right, girls, we need a plan. I've decided to enter the talent contest and I need the BFC to help me win. I'm going to sing "U & Me"—the latest Beat Boyz single.

Kaitlin.New.Girl: What a surprise! What do you need exactly?

Aliesha4eva: Kaitlin, as Designer, you're in charge of designing my outfit.

Kaitlin.New.Girl: Cool!

Aliesha4eva: Addison, as Events Organizer, can you make sure that the sound and lighting is exactly right?

AddisonSportsStar: Yes, boss. Whatever you say, boss.

Aliesha4eva: Noelle, as Secretary, I need you to get me a copy of the words to "U & Me" and to make sure I know it perfectly.

Calista100: What about me?

Aliesha4eva: As Treasurer, I need you to figure out how we're going to spend our winnings!!!

Send

Tuesday 4 pm

I got into school early this morning to sign up for the talent show. Even though the bell hadn't rung yet, a few people had already put their names on the list.

I grabbed a pen from my bag and scribbled my signature under "Performers." I heard a snicker behind me. It was Dina with two of her sidekicks, Mel and Kelly.

"Oh, look," said Dina. "Aliesha thinks she has a chance of winning the talent contest. How sweet. Has anyone pointed out to you that you actually need some talent to win, Aliesha?"

As Mel and Kelly cracked up laughing, Dina barged past me and added her name to the list. I walked away, cheeks flaming. Years from now, when I'm a famous singer, admired the world over for my amazing talent (hey, it could happen), they'll be sorry. Especially when I give my "MTV Most Talented Singer" acceptance speech. They won't be laughing then, I can tell you. In fact I might just write my acceptance speech now. Just so I'm ready.

MTV Most Talented
Singer Acceptance Speech

Wow! This is totally unexpected. I don't know what to say. I'd like to thank my family, in particular my mom, dad, and my twin sister, Noelle. I'd also like to thank the BFC—the best club in the world, without whose love, friendship, and support I wouldn't be standing in front of you today. I'd also like to thank Dina and her crew—Gianna, Sophie, Mel and Kelly. But I can't. Because these five girls have mocked, teased, and basically been mean to me and my pals almost every day at school. So it's no thanks to them that I stand in front of you, accepting this award as an amazingly talented and beautiful singer. I can only hope they think about what they've done, while I take this award back to my luxury ten-bedroom house, complete with Olympic-sized swimming pool. Thank you. Oh, and I'd also like to thank my boyfriend—the gorgeous Mickey Dean.

(Well, a girl can dream, can't she!)

Thursday 6 pm ✦ ✦

Rehearsing for this talent show (WHICH BY THE WAY IS TOMORROW NIGHT!!!!) has taken over my life. After all, I want to be the best I can possibly be, but my constant singing is driving Noelle crazy.

"I used to love 'u and me,'" she sighed, as I made her watch my routine one more time before we went to bed last night. "Now I'd be thrilled if I never heard it again."

I threw a pillow at her.

"Noelle! How could you?!" I replied. "This is one of the most meaningful songs ever written."

I'm not joking. It really is a cool song. It's all about finding someone really special and knowing your life won't be the same without them. The first two lines "I can't do this without you, without you nothing is true!" are totally haunting. It's SO catchy too—I even caught Dad humming it in the kitchen the other day.

I can't wait till tomorrow. I'm so excited.

Look out, Green meadow!
A star is about to be born!

80

Friday 4 pm

I feel sick. I'm sitting in the girls' bathroom writing in my diary and I can't stop shaking. I mean, I look great—Kait has totally outdone herself with the outfit. I'm wearing a gorgeous, polka-dot mini-dress over a long-sleeved top, striped leggings, cowboy boots, and a cute beanie to top it all off.

But I can't remember a single line of the song. As I was watching everyone else perform, I started to get butterflies in my tummy. A whole swarm of them. Can you even get a swarm of butterflies? Anyway, I don't feel great. But, the show must go on. . .

Friday 6:10 pm

I almost made a complete fool of myself in front of Chris Adams. After I came out of the bathroom, I went up to Ms. Street, our class teacher, who was backstage, organizing everyone.

"I can't go on," I said to her. "I can't do it!"

Ms. Street smiled at me reassuringly and patted my hand.

"Don't be silly, Aliesha. You'll be fine."

"I can't remember the song words," I said. "I'm not doing it, I'll make an idiot of myself."

Ms. Street fixed me with one of her best don't-mess-with-me glares.

"Aliesha Roberts, you are by far the most confident member of my class. If anyone can perform in this show, it's you," she said. "Now, you're the last act to go on stage. You have precisely five minutes to get it together."

Honestly, why can't teachers ever say things you want to hear, like:

1. Don't worry about getting good grades—it's enough having you as a pupil.

2. We're going on a school trip to Disney World.

3. Don't eat your lunch if you don't want it. There's plenty of ice cream and chocolate to pig out on later.

I decided to go to the bathroom (again) to calm my nerves. On the way, I knocked over a half-empty cardboard cup of coffee that one of the teachers had left on a table. It spilled down my dress. Now I looked like I'd wet myself. Great. Just GREAT!

"Don't cry," I told myself as I ran into the toilets. I splashed my face with water.

"Okay," I told myself, "I can do this." I brushed my hair, wiped off my leggings, reapplied my lip gloss, then walked to the side of the stage. Suddenly Noelle appeared next to me.

"I just wanted to wish you luck," she smiled. "From me and the rest of the BFC."

She took a closer look at me. "Aliesha? Are you okay? You don't look well."

"I don't think. . ." I stuttered.

"Oh, there you are!" Ms. Street interrupted, pushing me onto the stage, "You're on!"

As a spotlight shone on me, the music started and I opened my mouth to sing. But nothing came out! The audience started to shift uncomfortably in their seats. Someone snickered. Someone who sounded suspiciously like Dina.

Ms. Street started the music again. I felt tears starting to prick the back of my eyes. I took a deep breath, and managed to whisper the first two lines. There was no way I was going to get through the rest of the song. I was about to run off offstage when I heard a voice singing the next two lines again. Perfectly.

The voice sounded like mine, but it wasn't. Plus, it wasn't coming from me, but from the other side of the stage. I glanced around. It was Noelle! She walked onto the stage toward me, took my hand, and squeezed it.

"Come on, Aliesha," she whispered. "You can't let me do this on my own."

Suddenly the words and the dance routine came flooding back. I grinned at her and the two of us launched into the act. Noelle had watched me do it so many times that we were perfectly in sync. When we finished, the audience went crazy.

I could see the rest of our BFC buddies jumping up and down, whistling and cheering.

I hugged Noelle and the two of us ran offstage.

"That performance was inspired," gushed Ms. Street. "Pretending to be too scared to sing, then doing it as a duet. It really brought the meaning of the song to life. Good job!"

"I owe it all to Noelle," I grinned at my sister, who winked back at me.

"Well, don't go anywhere," said Ms. Street, nodding toward the stage. "The results are just about to be announced."

Chris Adams walked onstage.

"Well," he said. "I think you'll agree, it's been a wonderful night. Who'd have thought one small school could hold so much talent? Come on out, everyone!"

We all trooped out onto the stage, grinning as the audience went crazy, clapping and stamping their approval.

Chris Adams held his hands up. "But sadly, there can only be one winner. So without further ado, please give a huge round of applause to. . . Aliesha and Noelle Roberts!"

I stared at Noelle in disbelief, as everyone around us hugged us and slapped us on the back. Everyone except Dina and her crew, who were too busy muttering "Fix! Fix!" under their breath, that is.

As we made our way towards Chris Adams to receive the prize, I caught sight of Kaitlin, Addison, and Calista jumping up and down with excitement. I grinned at Noelle, who winked back. My best friends are just that...

the BEST!

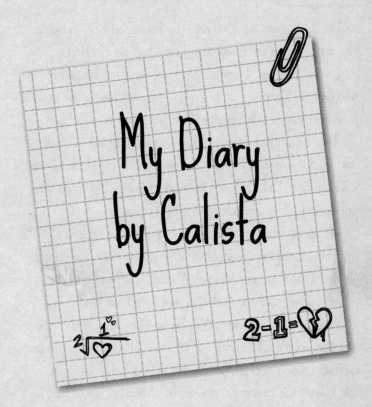

My Diary by Calista

$$2\sqrt{\overset{\heartsuit}{1}} \qquad 2-1=\heartsuit$$

Sunday 7 pm

I've just come back to my new house, after spending the afternoon with my new friend at my old house.

Ever since our families went on vacation together, me and Gianna Harris have been hanging out loads. We've got tons in common. Like pesky little sisters, for starters.

The fact that Gianna lives in our old house is kinda odd, and it's mega-freaky hanging out in my old bedroom with all her stuff there instead of mine, but once you get used to the weirdness, it's pretty cool.

We spent most of today singing along to Gianna's MP3 player and making up dance routines. Obviously, we were nowhere near as amazing as Aliesha and Noelle in the school talent contest, but still, we tried our best.

I managed to convince Aliesha and Noelle to put their winnings into a BFC bank. That way, if any emergencies crop up (e.g. a certain band's concert tickets going on sale), we won't have to do any of Aliesha's harebrained fund-raising schemes.

I told Gianna about the BFC and she looked kinda interested, like she was wondering if hanging out with the BFC would be more fun than hanging with Dina and her cronies...maybe I imagined it.

I still feel bad about keeping my friendship with Gianna a secret from the others. But they're convinced Gianna's mean, like her friend Dina, even though she's far from it. The only time I've kept a secret this big was when I found out we were moving to Canada, and that almost split the BFC up for good. I need to find a way to explain it to them.

Monday 5 pm

So I decided that I would tell the others about Gianna today. I mean, why CAN'T I choose which friends I have? Anyway, me, Kaitlin, Noelle, Addison, and Aliesha had just sat down in the cafeteria at lunchtime and I was totally getting ready to tell them, when Dina came stalking over.

"Look who it is," she sneered. "Aliesha Roberts and her freaky friends." I looked up and saw Gianna right at the back of the group, looking awkward.

Aliesha sighed. "What do you want, Dina?"

"Your table. This place is crammed full, and me and my friends want to sit together," Dina replied.

"Well, we're not moving," said Aliesha firmly.

"Come on, Dina, let's find somewhere else to sit," Gianna told her friend quietly.

"Is everything all right over here, girls?" It was Ms. Street, our teacher.

"Yes, everything's fine," Dina sulked, glaring at Aliesha, before storming off toward a table on the other side of the cafeteria. Mel and Sophie followed closely behind. I glanced across at Gianna, who was now sitting two tables away with Kelly, and sighed.

No way could I tell the others about me and Gianna now. If Aliesha found out I'd spent two minutes hanging out with one of Dina's gang she'd totally flip out. So much for not keeping secrets, huh?!

Thursday 4 pm

Aliesha and Noelle have just invited me and Addison over to their house on Saturday for pizza and a DVD. The thing is, I've already arranged to go to the movies with Gianna. I told Aliesha I couldn't go because I was visiting my Grandma, but I feel really bad about it. I hate keeping secrets and I hate lying to my friends, but I don't want to let Gianna down either. After all, she's a friend too.

Friday 6 pm

Gianna slipped a note into my bag as she walked past me on the way out of school this afternoon. The rest of Dina's gang and the other members of the BFC were too busy giving each other dirty looks to even notice. I had to wait until I got home to open it—Aliesha is such a gossip queen, if she'd spotted Gianna's note, she would have made a huge fuss.

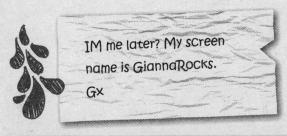

IM me later? My screen name is GiannaRocks.

Gx

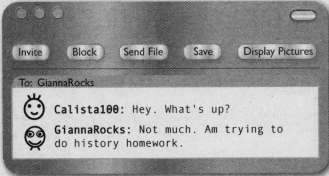

Invite   Block   Send File   Save   Display Pictures

To: GiannaRocks

Calista100: Hey. What's up?

GiannaRocks: Not much. Am trying to do history homework.

Ms. Street has given us this huge class project on the ancient Egyptians.

 Calista100: Me, too. I'm making a pyramid out of matchboxes.

 GiannaRocks: Cool idea!

 Calista100: What time's the film 2moro?

 GiannaRocks: 2:30. I had to tell an enormous lie to Dina about it.

 Calista100: Why?

 GiannaRocks: She asked me to go bowling at the same time.

 Calista100: Me, too!

 GiannaRocks: Seriously?

 Calista100: Well, no—not Dina. I had to tell my friends I couldn't see them because I was visiting my Grandma. I wish they'd all chill out.

 GiannaRocks: Fat chance.

 Calista100: You do still want to be friends, though, right?

GiannaRocks: Course. C u @ the movies! x

Send

Saturday 8 pm

Call it gut instinct but I totally knew my movie date with Gianna was going to end in disaster today.

We took our seats at the back of the theater and balanced our popcorn between us. It felt like we had loads to catch up on. Even though I see her every day in school, we can't exactly settle down for a good gossip with Aliesha and Dina watching.

I scooped up a handful of popcorn, giggling as Gianna did a stupid impression of Mr. Chester, our principal, and then froze. Aliesha, Noelle, and Addison had just started to walk up the steps toward me and Gianna. I tried to sink lower into my seat to hide, but eagle-eyed Aliesha spotted me.

"Calista!" she said, as she and the others came closer to our row.

I tried to speak but no sound came out.

"This must be your grandma," she added, jerking her head at Gianna. "Oh no, that's right, it's Gianna Harris."

"I couldn't...I mean...I didn't..." I tried to say.

"Forget it," Aliesha snapped. "We're not interested in hearing your traitor excuses."

"I'm not a traitor!" I said.

"What else would you call someone who blows off her best friends to go out with. . . " Aliesha fished around for the right word.

"The enemy?" suggested Addison.

"Exactly," said Aliesha, hooking arms with Noelle and Addison. "Come on, let's leave them alone. If you're such good friends, you're welcome to each other."

"Sorry," said Gianna, as we watched them walk away. "If I hadn't invited you here, that wouldn't have happened."

"You've got nothing to be sorry about. Why shouldn't I have other friends? There's no law against it," I finished.

After that, I was angry, upset, and guilty. Seriously not a good combo when it comes to enjoying a film. We had all argued before, but I really couldn't see how we were going to work things out this time. What right does Aliesha have to tell me who I can be friends with or not? I can be friends with whoever I want!

Monday 4 pm

I officially have no friends. Honestly, it's so bad, I almost wish we were living back in Canada.

I was mega-nervous going into school this morning, even though I'd totally practised what I was going to say.

I shouldn't have bothered, though—no one in the BFC is talking to me at all. I couldn't even find them in the cafeteria at lunchtime, so I left and sat on one of the benches outside the gym. After about ten minutes, I looked up and saw Gianna coming toward me.

"You can come over and hang out with us if you like," said Gianna, pointing toward Dina's gang on the other side of the yard. "They're cool," she said. "I asked them, and they don't mind." I decided it was better than sitting on my own, and followed her back to the group.

"Hiya," mumbled Sophie.

"Hey," said Kelly.

I nodded. "Where's, uh, Dina?" I asked nervously.

"She'll be back in a minute," said Mel. "She went to get her lip gloss."

We chatted kind of awkwardly for a few minutes. At least, that is, until Dina got back.

"You are kidding me!" she said, looking between Gianna

and me. "We're friends," said Gianna. "No one else minds."

"Well, I do," said Dina. "She's probably just here spying for that bunch of no-hopers she hangs around with."

Gianna tried to explain about Aliesha and the others ignoring me.

"Whatever, Gi," said Dina. "You're either friends with her or friends with us. You can't be both."

"That's not fair!" said Gianna.

"Choose," said Dina.

Gianna looked at me, and then back at Dina.

"I'm really sorry," she said to me eventually.

I didn't exactly mind. I mean, if I had to choose between one new friend and a whole bunch of old ones, I'd probably have done the same thing. The trouble was, I still didn't get why everyone seemed to think you could only have one or the other.

Wednesday 8 pm

With no BFC after school and no one to share IM gossip with, I asked Ms. Street if I could stay behind and work on my history project for a while.

My pyramid was almost finished and I'd decided to make a sphinx to go with it. Ms. Street said it would be fine, so I headed off to raid the art-supply closet. When I came back, I was surprised to find Kaitlin sitting in the classroom.

"Ms. Street went to do some marking in the teachers' lounge," she said, seeing me look around the room. "It's just us here."

I didn't really know what to say. I sat down at my desk and held up the pile of art supplies I was carrying.

"I'm making a sphinx," I said lamely.

Kaitlin showed me this amazing fake-gold bracelet she was working on.

"Ancient Egyptian jewelry," she said.

There was silence for a minute.

"I'm really sorry," we both said at the same time, and then laughed. The next thing I knew, we'd pushed our projects aside, and I was confiding everything to Kaitlin. How Gianna and I had made friends on holiday, how we'd been hanging out since we got back, and how difficult it was to keep it a secret.

Somehow, it was easier to tell one person than all four of my best friends at the same time.

Thursday 5:30 pm

http://www.bfcink.com

mail   Inbox (3)   Junk (2)   Drafts   Sent   Deleted   Folders   Calendar

From: Gianna Harris <GiannaRocks@star.com>

To: Calista100@bfc.com

Subject: Friends?

Verdana   10   **B** *I* U̲

Hi!

I feel horrible about everything that's happened, especially Dina making me choose between you two. Sometimes I wonder why I hang out with her. She can be totally bossy. I still want us to be friends outside of school if you do. Maybe we could get together on the weekend?

L8r,

Gianna x

Invite   Block   Send File   Save   Display Pictures

To: Calista100

Kaitlin.New.Girl: Have set up a BFC meeting @ mine, 2moro after school. Can u come? x

98

Friday 7:33 pm

When I got to Kaitlin's house tonight, the others were already there.

"Uh, what's she doing here?" Aliesha asked Kaitlin, as soon as I walked in.

I thought Kaitlin had told them I was coming and that they wanted to talk to me. Instead, she'd tricked them into showing up...

"Go on, Cal," said Kaitlin, shutting her bedroom door and leaning against it. "Tell them all that stuff you told me."

And so I did. I explained about the vacation, me hanging out at my old house (which is now Gianna's house), having to sneak around in secret...

"Just because I've got a new friend, doesn't mean we can't be best friends anymore," I finished. "I tried to tell you, honestly I did. I didn't want to keep it from you."

"When you think about it, all of us have got friends outside the BFC," Kaitlin continued. "Noelle does dog-training with Ben, Addison goes to the skate park with Elliot, and Aliesha's got loads of friends at dance class."

"It's not like you can have too many friends," I said, then added quickly, "I mean, best friends are different.

But Gianna's not my best friend, all of you are."

Noelle and Addison looked like they understood, but Aliesha was scowling. Addison nudged Aliesha playfully. "Who was it who told me I was being an idiot when I was jealous of Calista's new friend in Canada?"

"This is different!" Aliesha argued. "We saw Calista hanging out with Dina's gang!"

"So?" I was starting to feel annoyed. "Gianna only invited me over because you guys weren't speaking to me," I reminded her.

Noelle was frowning at Aliesha. "You don't want to be as shallow and petty as Dina, do you?"

Aliesha tried to frown back, but I could see her starting to smile. "OK! OK, Smartypants!"

They all came over and hugged me then, apologizing like crazy, while I did the same thing.

"I still can't believe you thought Calista would join Dina's gang," said Kaitlin, flopping down on one of her beanbags.

"As if!" said Aliesha.

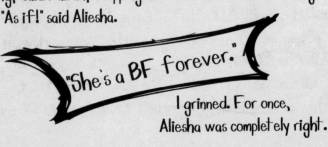

"She's a BF forever."

I grinned. For once, Aliesha was completely right.

MY DIARY BY ADDISON

Sunday 5:40 pm

I STILL DON'T THINK I CAN QUITE BELIEVE IT. CALISTA AND GIANNA, ONE OF DINA'S BEST FRIENDS, ARE BUDDIES! I MEAN, I TOTALLY UNDERSTAND HOW IT'S HAPPENED, WHAT WITH THEIR BABY SISTERS BEING FRIENDS. BUT I'M STILL GETTING OVER THE SHOCK. ANYWAY, I'M JUST GLAD THAT CALISTA WANTS TO BE PALS WITH US. FOR A HORRIBLE MOMENT, WE THOUGHT SHE MIGHT JOIN DINA AND HER CREW. HA, AS IF!

Monday 7 pm

I CANNOT BELIEVE WHAT I SAW AT THE SKATE PARK AFTER SCHOOL TODAY. I WENT WITH MY BROTHERS, JAKE AND JOSH, AND WE MET ELLIOT THERE (HE GETS CUTER EVERY TIME I SEE HIM). ANYWAY, WE WERE ALL TOTALLY AMAZED BY A GIRL NAMED NELLY. I'VE NEVER SEEN HER AT THE PARK BEFORE BUT I'VE HEARD OF HER, COS SHE'S THE BEST GIRL SKATER EVER! SHE'S ON SOME SORT OF SKATEBOARDING TOUR, TRYING OUT OUR RAMPS.

EVEN JAKE WAS IMPRESSED WITH NELLY'S SKILLS.

"IT'S AS IF SHE FEARS NOTHING," HE SAID, WATCHING HER KICK HER BOARD INTO THE AIR, FLIP IT 360 DEGREES, AND LAND ON IT PERFECTLY. EVERY TIME I TRY THAT TRICK, I FALL OVER.

And not only is Nelly super-talented, she's also really nice.

"Hey, Nelly," I said, when she stopped for a break, "do you mind if we watch you for a while?" I waved my arm in the direction of my brothers and Elliot.

"Sure," she smiled and then whispered, "just promise not to laugh at me if I mess up."

As if someone like Nelly would ever miss a trick. I think she was just trying to make me feel good. I mean, seriously, she did this amazing stunt (well, series of stunts, really) which I made a note of and stuck in my diary below so I can try it out.

1. First, pick up speed by skating through a tunnel, and then race up a ramp on the other side.

2. Next, jump in the air, twist the other way, and land backwards on your board.

3. Skate backwards before flipping the board around again, and land on it, this time facing forward.

4. Finally, flick the board up into the air and catch it with your left hand.

Piece of cake. NOT!

I told the gang about Nelly today.

"I think I saw her in a TV documentary on extreme sports, ages ago," Aliesha said.

"Really?" Calista giggled. "News flash. . .Aliesha Roberts watches something other than pop on TV."

"Oh, I think I might die of shock," Noelle sighed dramatically, clutching her chest.

"Ha de ha," Aliesha giggled, playfully punching Noelle on the arm. "There are many sides and talents to your better twin, missy. Now don't you forget it."

Just think, if I ever became as good as Nelly at skateboarding, I might be on TV one day too. And then maybe a group of cool girls, who just so happen to be in an amazing club, might be having this very same conversation, only about ME!!!

Okay, a bit far-fetched, I know. But everyone dreams, don't they?

I can't wait to go back to the skate park. I'm gonna see if Mom and Dad will let me practice most of this week and on Saturday too.

Friday 7:05 pm

My powers of persuasion worked! I've been allowed to skate almost every day this week after school.

Well, except for Tuesday, cos I had basketball practice then. I think Mom and Dad are even going to watch me skate tomorrow.

While I'm wowing my family with some cool tricks that I've picked up from Nelly (I hope), Aliesha and co. will be making up dance routines and giving each other makeovers. AGAIN! Seriously, if prancing around plastered in make-up was an Olympic sport, my fellow BFC members would all be gold medalists by now. I can't even bear to think about the amount of paint Noelle shoveled onto my face when I asked them to turn me into one of them.

I'm over that now, though.

Seriously, if I didn't have my sports to get me out of girly BFC sessions, I really don't know what I'd do.

mail   Inbox (3)   Junk (2)   Drafts   Sent   Deleted   Folders   Calendar

From:	Noelle Roberts < SmileyNoelle@bfc.com
To:	Kaitlin.New.Girl@bfc.com, AddisonSportsStar@bfc.com, Calista100@bfc.com, Aliesha4eva@bfc.com
Subject:	BFC agenda (i.e. stuff we're going to say and do)

Verdana   10   **B** *I* U

<u>Place of Meeting</u>: Addison's house at 2 pm

<u>Members Present</u>:

Noelle

Aliesha

Kaitlin

Calista

Addison (obviously)

<u>Discussion one</u>: Addison's fractured ankle

Things required for meeting:

• "Get Well Soon" card

• Magazines

• Candy

• Um... anything else people give to the needy.

Yours sincerely,

Noelle

BFC Secretary

Invite | Block | Send File | Save | Display Pictures

To: Aliesha4eva, SmileyNoelle, Calista100, Kaitlin.New.Girl

AddisonSportsStar: I am not and never have been NEEDY, thank you very much.

Kaitlin.New.Girl: Can you walk on your left foot?

AddisonSportsStar: No.

Calista100: Can you walk without the aid of crutches?

AddisonSportsStar: No.

Aliesha4eva: Can you slip a shoe over the cast on your left foot?

AddisonSportsStar: NO!

SmileyNoelle: HA! You are needy, Addison Jackson, and we at the BFC know when we are needed!

Send

SUNDAY 7 pm

THE BFC ROCKS! BUT MY ANKLE DOESN'T...
I TRIED TO DO NELLY'S MOVE AT THE SKATE PARK ON

SATURDAY. I MANAGED TO GET THE FIRST PART, BUT THEN, WHEN I TRIED TO JUMP IN THE AIR AND TWIST BACKWARDS, I MISSED MY BOARD ON THE WAY DOWN. MY ANKLE MADE A LOUD CRUNCH NOISE WHEN IT HIT THE GROUND.

IT HURTS SO MUCH. I HAD TO GO TO THE HOSPITAL AND EVERYTHING. AFTER MY X-RAY, THE DOCTOR DISCOVERED THAT I'D FRACTURED MY ANKLE. I CAN'T SKATE FOR ABOUT SIX WEEKS. NO SWIMMING EITHER. NO BASKETBALL. NO TENNIS. NO SPORTS! I WAS MORE UPSET BY THAT THAN ANYTHING ELSE. I ACTUALLY CRIED WHEN THE DOCTOR TOLD ME. UGH! AND IN FRONT OF MOM, DAD, MY BROTHERS, JAKE AND JOSH, AND JAKE'S FRIENDS, BEN AND ELLIOT, TOO. TOTALLY UNCOOL.

NOELLE ORGANIZED A BFC MEETING AT MY HOUSE EARLIER TO TRY AND CHEER ME UP. ALIESHA BROUGHT ME SOME SKATER MAGS TO READ (ALTHOUGH I CAN'T BEAR TO THINK ABOUT SKATING RIGHT NOW), ALONG WITH THE LATEST ISSUE OF "THE JUICE" OF COURSE, AND KAITLIN HAD MADE ME A GET WELL CARD. CALISTA AND NOELLE POLISHED OFF MOST OF THE CANDY, THOUGH.

BUT WHAT AM I GOING TO DO WITHOUT MY SPORTS? SIX WEEKS IS A L-O-N-G TIME. FOREVER, IN FACT.

Monday 2 pm

I. AM. SO. BORED! Mom said I should stay home today while I learn how to walk properly with my crutches. Properly? How can anyone walk properly with crutches? And my foot still kind of hurts a little. I used to think that having a day off school would be awesome.

But I just wish I was in school with the others, fooling around. . . I mean working hard. I'd even be pleased to see Dina's face right now, that's how bored I am.

Tuesday 4 pm

I went back to school today. Walking around on crutches is a sport in itself. Seriously, I had no idea how tiring it would be to hop around all day long. Everything is so slow when you have crutches. I have to wait for everyone else to leave the classroom or assembly before I can move anywhere.

And then, to make matters worse, I found out that my place in the basketball team is going to be taken by Dina's pal, Sophie. It's SO unfair.

Thursday 7:25 pm

I'M A LITTLE FASTER ON MY CRUTCHES NOW. AND I'VE ALSO DISCOVERED THAT IF ONE OF DINA'S GANG (WITH THE EXCEPTION OF GIANNA, OF COURSE) GETS IN MY WAY, I CAN KIND OF PROD THEM WITH MY CRUTCH. ACCIDENTALLY ON PURPOSE, OF COURSE.

"ADDISON, YOU HAVE GOT TO STOP DOING THAT," CALISTA WHISPERED WHEN SHE SAW ME TRIP DINA WITH ONE OF MY CRUTCHES. DINA GLARED AT ME AS SHE TOOK AN EXTRA STEP FORWARD TO STEADY HERSELF. "OOPS, SORRY, DINA," I SAID INNOCENTLY. "I DIDN'T SEE YOU THERE."

CALISTA CAME BACK TO MY HOUSE AFTER SCHOOL. SHE SAID I NEEDED SOMEONE TO KEEP ME COMPANY WHILE JAKE AND JOSH WENT SWIMMING. PLUS, SHE HAD A GREAT SPORTS QUIZ TO GIVE ME THAT SHE'D COMPILED ESPECIALLY TO HELP ME KEEP BUSY. IT'S SO COOL, CHECK THIS OUT. . .

> Question – Which two tennis players have a mom named Brandi?
> Answer – Venus and Serena Williams

I DID NOT KNOW THAT. SOME ARE REALLY HARD! CALISTA MUST HAVE SPENT HOURS DOING IT FOR ME. SHE CAN TOTALLY BE MY DEPUTY EVENTS ORGANIZER ANYTIME WITH QUIZZES LIKE THIS!!!

Friday 7 pm

To:AddisonSportsStar

Aliesha4eva: Hey, Addy! R u free 2moro?

AddisonSportsStar: Um, let me check my datebook. Oh, it looks like I might be stuck at home with a cast on my foot for company.

Aliesha4eva: Cool, I take it that's a "Yes" then. C u l8r, alligator. x

Send

Saturday 5 pm

ALIESHA'S JUST BEEN OVER WITH EVEN MORE MAGS. WELL, ACTUALLY, ONE MAG REALLY, JUST LOTS OF BACK ISSUES. CAN YOU GUESS WHICH MAG? YEP, "THE JUICE." I DON'T MIND, THOUGH, ANYTHING TO KEEP MY MIND OFF DOING SPORTS. I THOUGHT IT WAS JUST A GOSSIP MAG, BUT THERE ARE TIPS ON MAKE-UP, HAIR, CLOTHES. SERIOUSLY, I HAD NO IDEA THAT CHOPPY BOBS ARE IDEAL FOR PEOPLE WITH LONG

FACES. BUT I DON'T HAVE A LONG FACE, DO I? AARGH, I'M
TURNING INTO MY BFC PALS.

> **Question - How many lanes would you find
> in an Olympic swimming pool?
> Answer - Eight**

I TOTALLY KNEW THAT. I AM SO GETTING THE HANG
OF CALISTA'S SPORTS QUIZ.

SUNDAY 5:55 pm

ONLY #1!

I CAN'T BELIEVE I HAVEN'T DONE ANYTHING SPORTY THIS
WEEKEND. BUT YOU KNOW WHAT? ALIESHA, KAITLIN, NOELLE,
AND CALISTA HAVE KEPT ME SO BUSY, I HAVEN'T REALLY
THOUGHT ABOUT IT.

ON SATURDAY, KAITLIN INVITED ALL OF US OVER TO HER
HOUSE TO WATCH THE TEEN FLICK, "THE CLIQUES."

THEN, TODAY, CALISTA CAME TO MINE AND BROUGHT
ME SOME MORE SPORTS QUIZZES. I DIDN'T KNOW SHE KNEW
SO MUCH ABOUT SPORTS—BUT SHE SAYS SHE'S FOUND THIS
REALLY GOOD INTERNET SITE THAT'S GOT LOADS OF
QUESTIONS ON IT. I'VE ONLY JUST MANAGED TO FINISH THE
FIRST QUIZ SHE GAVE ME AND NOW I'VE GOT THREE MORE
TO DO!

TUESDAY 4 pm

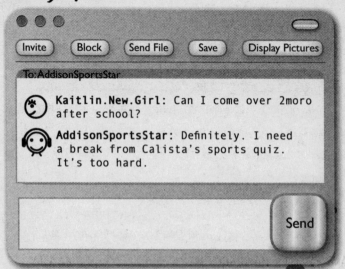

● ● ●

(Invite)   (Block)   (Send File)   (Save)   (Display Pictures)

To:AddisonSportsStar

✿ **Kaitlin.New.Girl:** Can I come over 2moro after school?

😊 **AddisonSportsStar:** Definitely. I need a break from Calista's sports quiz. It's too hard.

Send

WEDNESDAY 8 pm

KAITLIN IS JUST SO TALENTED! GOOD THING WE CHOSE HER TO BE THE BFC DESIGNER. SHE BROUGHT HER SKETCH PAD AND SOME COLORED PENCILS WITH HER YESTERDAY. AND GUESS WHAT WE DID? GUESS, GUESS! WE CREATED A DESIGN FOR MY SKATEBOARD. WE SCRIBBLED SOME IDEAS IN KAITLIN'S SKETCH PAD. SHE'S GONNA WORK THEM UP ONTO SOME BIGGER PAPER, THEN, LATER IN THE WEEK, WE'LL PUT THE DESIGNS ON MY BOARD. IT'S GONNA LOOK SO COOL!

Monday 4:30 pm

I'VE SPENT THE LAST TWO DAYS WITH NOELLE, HELPING HER TRAIN MAX. HE IS SO CUTE!

"TRAINING A PUPPY IS VERY TIME-CONSUMING," NOELLE TOLD ME. "YOU HAVE TO BE PATIENT. AND VERY STERN."

SHE ADDED THE LAST BIT WHEN SHE SAW ME OFFER MAX A DOGGY TREAT FOR DOING NOTHING AT ALL. WELL, HIS BIG BROWN EYES MADE ME DO IT!

Monday—three weeks later

I CAN'T BELIEVE IT! THE DOCTOR SAID I CAN HAVE MY CAST REMOVED IN FIVE DAYS. YAY!

Saturday 4 pm

IT'S OFF!!! NO MORE CAST. NO MORE ITCHY ANKLE. IT'S BACK TO SPORTS! I REALLY DON'T THINK I WOULD HAVE BEEN ABLE TO GET THROUGH THIS WITHOUT MY PALS (WE'RE ALL GOING TO KAITLIN'S LATER TO CELEBRATE).

I'VE EVEN PERSUADED MOM TO TAKE ME TO THE SKATE PARK TOMORROW. AND I'VE PROMISED NOT TO TRY ANY DANGEROUS TRICKS. WELL, NOT THIS WEEK ANYWAY. . .

My diary
by Noelle

115

Saturday 12:30 pm

It's amazing what you can learn at a sleepover. Seriously. Check this out. . .

Things I learned at last night's sleepover...

1) When two boys (i.e. Jake and Ben) crash your sleepover because their camping trip went wrong, you need about three times the amount of food.

2) It's best to hide some snacks where they can't find them or they will polish off everything.

3) When two boys crash your sleepover, truth or dare is not the ideal game to play, especially if you have a massive crush on one of them (i.e. Ben).

4) When it is your turn to fess up the name of your crush and he is actually sitting right next to you, don't blush as red as the planet of Mars and croak "I'll take a dare!" in the voice of a frog.

5) If you think that asking for a dare is the safest option, think again! Or else your so-called friend Addison might dare you to switch places with your twin sister for a whole day!!!

"It isn't that bad, Noelle," said Kaitlin through a mouthful of toothpaste.

I looked at our reflections in the mirror above Addison's bathroom sink.

"So, like the quietest person in the world, i.e. me, isn't going to have any trouble pretending to be the loudest girl in the whole class, i.e. Aliesha?"

Kaitlin grinned a toothpastey grin. "Well. . ." she said.

"Egggagtly!" I cried with my toothbrush in my mouth.

"Maybe you could go to a hypnotist!" Kaitlin said after a minute.

She took off her pendant and swung it backwards and forwards.

"You are going to sleeeeeeeep," she cooed. "And when you wake up you will be Alieeeesha. You will know exactly what to say to boys, you'll shout out what you think in front of everyone, and you'll never ever blush agaaaaaain!"

I stared at her, my cheeks puffed out with toothpaste froth. Then I kind of giggled and

spluttered at the same time and toothpaste shot out of my mouth at the speed of light and splattered all over Ben's T-shirt. UGH!!! I looked up at him in horror. Why did he have to push the bathroom door open right at the crucial moment? Why did I have to spit all over him? WHY OH WHY?

After I'd blushed the color of a zillion tomatoes and Ben had laughed and gone to change his T-shirt, Kaitlin looked at me and sighed.

"You're right," she said. "It's going to take a miracle to convince everyone you're Aliesha."

Saturday 5:35 pm

mail   Inbox (3)   Junk (2)   Drafts   Sent   Deleted   Folders   Calendar

From:	Addison Jackson < AddisonSportsStar@bfc.com >
To:	KaitlinNewGirl@bfc.com, SmileyNoelle@bfc.com, Calista100@bfc.com, Aliesha4eva@bfc.com
Subject:	Noelle's dare

Verdana   10   **B**   *I*   <u>U</u>

Hi Clubbers!

After last night's game of truth or dare, there was only one member who dared to dare. And that, my friends, was Noelle!
As the darer of the dare, it's my duty to set out the rules.

So here they are.

The rules of the dare:

1) Noelle must pretend to be Aliesha for one whole day.

2) If anyone guesses what's going on, Noelle has to pretend to be Aliesha for an extra day.

3) Noelle has to do the dare on a school day.

And that's it! Tee-hee, this is going to be SO much fun.
See you all a bit later!!!

BFC forever!

Addison x

Sunday 2 pm

Just had a manic morning of Alieshafication. Everyone came over and we all wrote down what we thought made Aliesha, Aliesha. Then we all wrote down what made me, me. And then everyone started talking at once.

"Okay, Noelle. When you look at people, don't lower your head and look up at them through your eyelashes," said Calista.

"I don't do that," I gasped.

"YES, YOU DO!" everyone giggled together.

"It's the classic Noelle look," smiled Kaitlin.

"You've got to learn the Aliesha look," said Addison. "It kind of goes like this," she squared her shoulders and stared me in the eye, unblinkingly.

"I don't do that!" cried Aliesha.

"YES, YOU DO!" we all yelled.

It went on like that for a while. Then they got me to follow Aliesha around the room, copying her walk. Next, I had to say embarrassing things without blushing, so I could practice having

Aliesha-like nerves of steel. By the end of lunchtime,
I practically felt like a different person.

Still not sure I can convince the world I'm my
sister, though!

Sunday 5.30 pm

HEE! HEE! Guess what? I've just been talking
to Aliesha and she's got an even better idea. She
figures we should both switch places—which totally
makes sense, since we can't both go to school being
her—can we? So on Tuesday, she's going to be me
and I'm going to be her and we're not even going to
tell the rest of the BFC what we are doing.

Now that it's a twin thing, it seems like much more
fun than it did before. I'm still nervous but it's nice
to know that we're doing the dare together.

Monday 8 pm

Eeek!
I'm going to be Aliesha tomorrow!!!!!!!!!!!!!!!!!!!!!!

Tuesday 5:39 pm (the day of the switch) ♡

Aliesha shook me awake half an hour early today.

"Noelle! Wake up. We need to get into character," she yelled in my ear.

We raced around each other's rooms, getting dressed in each other's clothes.

I tried to teach Aliesha to blush at the same time but it didn't work. Eventually she resorted to holding her breath, but even then her face didn't get very red.

"It doesn't matter, sis," said Aliesha. "It's not like you walk around with a permo blush."

"Well, it feels like I do," I sighed.

"You're too hard on yourself—that's your problem," Aliesha said as she came toward me with her lipstick.

"I can't wear lipstick to school!" I yelped.

"Baloney!" Aliesha replied. "I wear it every day. It's subtle so I get away with it. Come here."

By the time Aliesha was finished, I seriously didn't recognize my reflection. Even Mom couldn't tell us apart. She sliced a banana into Aliesha's cereal bowl, much to Aliesha's disgust.

Everyone knows that Aliesha totally hates bananas. I grinned across the table at Aliesha and gave her a wink. If we could fool Mom, we could fool the BFC.

"I bet nobody guesses that you're me and I'm you," Aliesha giggled as we left the house.

"Well, they'd better not because then I'll have to repeat the dare," I said, rearranging Aliesha's backpack on my shoulder.

"Don't stress. It'll be cool," Aliesha said, oozing with confidence.

"Listen, Aliesha, don't go talking to anyone pretending to be me. . ." I began.

"Duh! Isn't that the whole point?" she laughed.

"I mean, don't try to fix things for me. . . don't try to. . ."

"Fix you up with Ben?" Aliesha finished. "Don't worry. I won't go talking to Ben."

When we got to school, the first challenge was meeting the other Clubbers in our classroom before the morning bell.

My heart was totally racing when I pulled back Aliesha's chair and slipped behind her desk.

"Hey!" I said, looking around at the girls in an Aliesha-ish manner. "What's up?"

Calista offered around some chocolate and Addison started talking about some baseball game.

"If that gorgeous shortstop isn't playing, I'm not interested," I said, going into Aliesha mode. "Baseball is boresome."

Aliesha-Noelle gave me a look of admiration. It was SO the kind of thing she would say!!!

It was pretty funny pretending to be each other in class, and after a while I started having fun. When Ms. Street asked us questions, I yelled out the answers at the top of my voice, just like Aliesha does. I gnawed the end of my pen, just like Aliesha does, and I joked around as much as I could. But lunchtime was the real challenge. Aliesha almost blew our cover when she started singing a Beat Boyz song in front of Addison in a very un-Noelle-ish way, but luckily she remembered just in time and quickly shut up before Addison noticed anything unusual.

The afternoon shot past and soon we were piling out of the school grounds. Aliesha winked at me when I caught her eye.

"We rock," Aliesha mouthed silently to me as we linked arms with the other BF Clubbers. I couldn't believe that they hadn't guessed Aliesha and I had switched places. When we got to the bus stop, I realized I'd left Aliesha's sneakers behind, so I told the others to go on without me, and made my way back to school, which was when I saw Ben.

I can't remember much of the conversation because my brain has actually frozen with shock, but it went something like this. . .

Action Replay of a Conversation Between Me and Ben Michelson:

Ben started the convo by saying this:

Hi, Aliesha! Can I talk to you for a sec?

So, me being Aliesha said:

Yeah, cool. What's going down?

125

Then Ben said:

> Um. I kind of wanted to ask you about Noelle. You know we've been hanging out with the dogs and stuff and. . .well. . .I was talking to her this afternoon. . .

Me, not being Aliesha very well, said:

> WHAT? Seriously? I can't believe her! She promised she wouldn't.

(The shock of finding out that Aliesha was talking to Ben while pretending to be me, without me even knowing, totally made me forget to be Aliesha-ish.)

Ben (confused) said:

> What do you mean? What did Aliesha—I mean Noelle. . . what did Noelle promise?

So I said:

> Oh, er, it's cool. Don't worry. Like, whatever. So you were saying?

And Ben said:

> Well. . . I kind of like Noelle and I wondered if you knew if she liked me.

I AM NOT JOKING! HE SERIOUSLY SAID THAT!

I think I'm going to faint. But first I am going to yell at Aliesha for talking to Ben!!!

Tuesday 7:20 pm

To: Aliesha4eva, SmileyNoelle, Calista100, Kaitlin.New.Girl

AddisonSportsStar: Hey guys! 2day was hilarious. You both totally rock as each other.

KaitlinNewGirl: You didn't fool us though.

Calista100: We guessed you'd switched places right away. Even Ben guessed!

Send

"WHAAAAAAT!" screeched Aliesha, as she read the gang's IMs. "I seriously can't believe they

127

double-tricked our trick back on us. They totally knew all along!"

I stared at my twin with my mouth open. Ben knew? BEN KNEW???!!! BEN KNEW?????? ?????????!!!!!!!!!!!!!!!!!!!

My brain started whirring like a washing machine. If Ben had guessed that I was Aliesha and Aliesha was me, then he must have known he was talking to me when he said that he liked me.

I think I am having a heart attack.

Wednesday 6:56 pm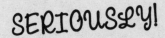

Deep breaths. Okay. Be cool. Be calm. Coolandcalm. I can't be calm!!! I can't! I can't! Like, this is the least calm moment of my life. Seriously! Okay. Okay. Sooooo. . . . . . .

Ben was waiting for us at the corner this morning. And he asked to MEET ME.

Then, after school, he asked me out. HE ASKED ME OUT! HE ASKED ME OUT!

SERIOUSLY!

But I had to check that Addison was cool with it all, since she liked Ben too and I wouldn't want her to be upset.

And when I asked she said, "Yes!" and gave me a hug. YAY! So then I went and found Ben and said, "Yes!" and we are going to the movies on Saturday night! La! Laa! Laaa! Laaaaa! Laaaaaaa! Laaaaaaaaaa!

Noelle and Ben
4eva!

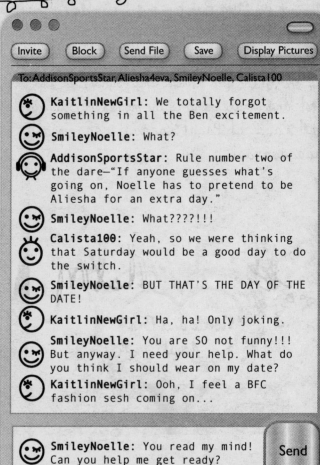

● ● ●   ⊖

(Invite) (Block) (Send File) (Save) (Display Pictures)

To: AddisonSportsStar, Aliesha4eva, SmileyNoelle, Calista100

KaitlinNewGirl: We totally forgot something in all the Ben excitement.

SmileyNoelle: What?

AddisonSportsStar: Rule number two of the dare—"If anyone guesses what's going on, Noelle has to pretend to be Aliesha for an extra day."

SmileyNoelle: What????!!!

Calista100: Yeah, so we were thinking that Saturday would be a good day to do the switch.

SmileyNoelle: BUT THAT'S THE DAY OF THE DATE!

KaitlinNewGirl: Ha, ha! Only joking.

SmileyNoelle: You are SO not funny!!! But anyway. I need your help. What do you think I should wear on my date?

KaitlinNewGirl: Ooh, I feel a BFC fashion sesh coming on...

SmileyNoelle: You read my mind! Can you help me get ready?

Send

130

Seriously, when can they? So excited!!!

My Diary

by Kaitlin

How much fun are makeovers?! Seriously, I could do this all day long. Me, Aliesha, Calista, and Addison have just finished transforming Noelle from cute babe to gorgeous girlfriend. Ben won't know what's hit him when our starry-eyed BFC secretary meets him for their hot date this afternoon.

Earlier today, Noelle and the others trooped over here, all ready for the makeover. Aliesha had picked out an outfit for Noelle to wear but, I mean, did Aliesha and Noelle learn ANYTHING during their swap?! Okay, I know that 50s-style strapless dresses are cool—and very Aliesha—but they are SO not Noelle. Like I said to the twins when I spied the outfit in question:

"You don't want Ben to think you two have switched places again, do you?"

Luckily, Noelle was wearing a plain top with her skinny jeans. In a millisecond, I had transformed it into a cool 70s-style disco-diva T-shirt. Teamed with my sparkly silver pumps and Aliesha's lip gloss and clear mascara, Noelle looked like an even better version of herself. Perfect for a date at the movies!

"Wow!" said Aliesha, admiring her twin sister with pride. "Our work here is done. You are good to go."

"Thanks, guys," said Noelle, blushing, "I'll give you the lowdown later. Wish me luck."

sunday 5 pm

Invite   Block   Send File   Save   Display Pictures

To: Kaitlin.New.Girl, Calista100, AddisonSportsStar, SmileyNoelle

Aliesha4eva: Noelle's in lo-o-ove, Noelle's in lo-o-ove…

SmileyNoelle: Am not.

Aliesha4eva: You are too. You've had this dreamy expression on your face ever since your date with Ben.

KaitlinNewGirl: Yay! Go Noelle. Our very own BFC romance. Finally!

Send

To tell the truth, I really thought Noelle and Ben would have gotten together weeks ago. Maybe even before Dad and Jen got married. But the course of true love never runs smoothly, as Katie would say.

I guess I can talk. Nothing's really happened between me and Jake since our little dance at Dad's wedding.

It would be too weird if anything had. Whenever I start getting gooey over Addison's older brother, she makes a face and groans, "Ew!"

I'll just have to keep my crush-y thoughts to myself, which is hard. Now that Noelle has gotten together with Ben, Jake is hanging around the BFC more than ever. And with the end of the semester coming up, I'm going to have to find a way to keep my feelings to myself during summer vacation—which, as the club's official secret spiller, is going to be a mammoth challenge.

monday 7 pm

I can't believe there are only two weeks left before school's out. Every year, a class is chosen to put on a show, and this year, it's ours. We have fifty dollars to spend on the outfits—which means mass-customization alert! Seriously, Aliesha can spend that amount on a purse, let alone several outfits for a show.

"Does anyone have any ideas for themes?" Ms. Street asked the class.

"Ooh, I know," said Aliesha, "we could do a fashion show. Kaitlin is amazing at styling outfits, Addison's great at planning events, Calista is great with budgets, Noelle is SO organized, she'll make sure everything runs smoothly, and I could be the host!"

Dina Harf let out a loud groan.

"Oh, puh-lease," she sighed. "Just what we need, the BF Dweebs in charge."

Ms. Street clapped her hands together and drowned out Dina's grumbles. "That sounds like a great idea, Aliesha, but the whole class has to participate in this project, too."

"Well," added Noelle, "maybe everyone else can be part of the backstage crew and either help with lighting, music, ticket sales..."

"Uh, you're forgetting one thing," Dina interrupted rudely. "Duh, the models?! You know, the people who are supposed to be wearing the outfits. Did I tell you, I once modeled for an agency?"

"Yeah, for ugly people," Addison snorted.

Dina is actually fairly pretty, but I wasn't looking forward to creating an outfit for her.

"If it's going to be a real fashion show," I said, thinking quickly, "then maybe we should have real models in it."

I went on to explain that my older sister was a magazine journalist and she could probably pull some strings to find a few models to help out. Obviously, I haven't asked Katie this yet, but I'm sure it will be okay. My sister is the BEST!

So, it's official. We're putting on a fashion show, featuring Designs à la Kaitlin. Everything HAS to go perfectly.

monday 7:30 pm

> Number of things going perfectly so far = none.
> Number of models in the fashion show = none.
> Number of sisters ruining my life = one.

"But why not?" I whined over the phone to Katie a minute ago. "Why can't you help me out this time?"

In the past, Katie has wrangled us tickets to see The Beat Boyz in concert, after we'd given the money we raised for them to the Brookbanks Dog Rescue Center. And, more recently, she's managed to score some press passes to see Mickey Dean's movie premiere.

So why can't she get us a few models? I mean, how hard can it be?!

"Because I'm a celeb journalist," Katie told me, exasperated. "I'm not a fashion editor. I can give you the names of some model agencies. Just call them up and ask if any of the models on their books are willing to strut their stuff for your fashion show for free."

I could tell by Katie's tone of voice that THAT was unlikely. Hrrmph!

tuesday 4 pm

Katie was right. The model agencies said no. Apparently, all their models are booked up for the next couple of months. What are we going to do? We can't have a fashion show without any models!!!

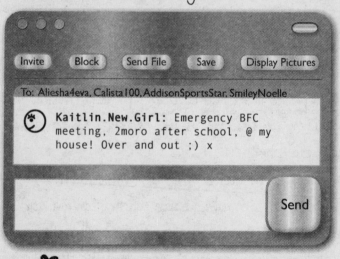

Invite   Block   Send File   Save   Display Pictures

To: Aliesha4eva, Calista100, AddisonSportsStar, SmileyNoelle

Kaitlin.New.Girl: Emergency BFC meeting, 2moro after school, @ my house! Over and out ;) x

Send

wednesday 7 pm 💙

| mail | Inbox (3) | Junk (2) | Drafts | Sent | Deleted | Folders | Calendar |

From: Noelle Roberts < SmileyNoelle@bfc.com >

To: Kaitlin.New.Girl@bfc.com, AddisonSportsStar@bfc.com, Calista100@bfc.com, Aliesha4eva@bfc.com

Subject: Minutes for Emergency BFC Meeting

| Verdana | | 10 | **B** | *I* | <u>U</u> |

<u>Place of Meeting</u>: Kaitlin's house, Kaitlin's bedroom.

<u>Members Present</u>: Noelle, Kaitlin, Aliesha, Addison, Calista

<u>Main Discussion:</u> Models for the school fashion show

<u>Conclusion:</u> We need some. ASAP.

<u>Action:</u> Addison's going to ask her brothers and their pals to be the boy models, and Calista's going to ask Gianna and her friends (which means Dina, too—aargh) to be the girl models.

Well, we are desperate!!!

Yours sincerely,

Noelle

BFC Secretary

239

Number of things going perfectly so far = none.
Oh, okay, maybe one. We have our models now. . .
Number of models in the fashion show = ten
(five boys and five girls). Addison begged Jake, Ben,
Elliot, Josh, and his pal, Ned, to take part.
Number of divas ruining EVERYTHING = one.

"Patches are SO last year," Dina groaned, when
I presented her with some customized jeans to wear
in the show. I'd spent ages sewing some cute patches
I'd made onto the denim fabric in art class. Luckily,
Aliesha came to my rescue.

"Well, we can thank our lucky stars that you're not
the fashion designer," she said, waving the style section
of "The Juice" magazine in Dina's face. "It says here
that patches are hot, right now."

Luckily, Dina didn't give me too much trouble after
that. I even caught her and Sophie adding some extra

patches to their denim outfits when I wasn't looking. Thankfully, I'm not the fussy kind. Besides, there's no point in causing a fuss. Everything HAS to go smoothly if I want to to finish all my designs in time for the show next Friday.

tuesday 7 pm

I just HAVE to write down the latest events. . . I finally finished customizing the outfits on Sunday evening and brought them into school for Dina and her cronies to try on for the dress rehearsal yesterday.

Dina was still yanking on a pair of jeans that I'd customized, when I left the school with Addison and Calista at the end of the day. Aliesha and Noelle were in the auditorium, practicing Aliesha's speech.

Anyway, I went into school a little earlier this morning to check everything was ready for the show.

The outfits were there...just not the way I'd left them. Most of the outfits had huge rips in the material and little tears down the sides. There was no way I would

141

be able to patch them up in time for the show.

Who would do such a thing? What kind of person would want to ruin the end-of-year show? Dina! It had to be! She was the last person in class yesterday.

I took a deep breath so that I could confront her in a clear and controlled way.

"You r-r-ruined m-my outfits," I sobbed uncontrollably, as soon as she got there.

"Wh-what?" Dina replied, looking puzzled. "I haven't done anything. I LOVE the outfits. I folded them up and placed them back in the bag last night."

"Uh-oh," said Aliesha rushing to the pile of outfits that I'd thrown across the floor. "Me and Noelle took them home last night so that we could finish writing my speech around the designs."

"The holes look like Max's nibbles," Noelle added tearfully. "He must have chewed them while I was sleeping last night. Oh, Kait, I'm so sorry. We were in such a rush to get to school this morning that we threw the outfits into the bag. We didn't think to check them."

"It's okay," I sniffed again. "I still have my sketches. I just don't think I can fix them on my own by Friday."

"We'll help," said Aliesha.

"Since it's all our fault anyway," Noelle added quietly.

"We'll help too," said Calista and Addison.

"And we can help sew more patches on," Dina added, looking around at her cronies for support. It totally took me by surprise. Had Dina lost her marbles? Well, I guess fashion can change a person's appearance, but I had NO idea it performed personality transplants too.

friday 9 pm

Number of fashion shows that went perfectly = one. Ms. Street thinks it was the best class show EVER.

Number of totally cute guy models = one. Jake looked so hot in the T-shirt I customized for him.

Number of times I had to pinch myself that Dina the Diva might be nearly nice after all = a million.

Number of best friends I want to have forever = four. The BFC totally rocks. At makeovers, at fashion, and most of all, at friendship!

143

BFC ink.

best friends Club. ink
Stick Together.
Friends Forever!

Hang out with your BFFs!

Be yourself!

SHARE SECRETS.

Look for
Best Friends Club, Ink.
Dolls, Toys and Accessories
for even More BFF Fun!